DEADLY NOEL

Strong Women, Extraordinary Situations
Book Five

To *Mom*

From
Gaile
2015

Margaret Daley

Deadly Noel
Copyright © 2015 Margaret Daley

http://www.margaretdaley.com/

ONE

Someone was watching her. She could feel it.

Kira Davis lifted her gaze to scan the grocery aisles in front of her. Nothing. She slowly turned. Her heartbeat accelerated, her palms damp with perspiration.

That was when she saw him. He leaned back against the counter, his jean clad legs crossed at the ankles, his arms folded over his chest. His silver-tarnished gaze drilled into her. Beneath his black Stetson, his expression was hard, unrelenting—dangerous. Three words that applicably described Gabriel Michaels, a man she'd sent to prison.

Help! He's after me.
Gabriel is...

Marcie screamed. The line went dead.

Her best friend's slurred plea, left on Kira's voicemail the day Marcie died, echoed through her mind, throwing her back to the day the nightmare began, the town still locked in its grip.

Gabriel pushed away from the counter and sauntered toward her. She hadn't thought it possible for her heart to increase its rapid beat, but it did. Dizzy, she gripped her shopping cart, determined to stand her ground. Fear tangled with an emotion she couldn't quite define as the man approached her.

His frosty gaze pierced through her as though she didn't exist.

Her mouth went dry.

She stiffened and swallowed several times, her chin tilted at a defiant angle while she returned his intense look. Her determination not to be intimidated solidified in the pit of her stomach.

She would never forget how he had looked at her the day the judge had pronounced his sentence. Gabriel had swung around, his gray eyes locking with hers across the short distance in the courtroom. Nothing, no one else mattered. She was alone in the world, stripped of all civilization, only the essence of life at its primeval core important. That was the moment she'd begun to doubt the verdict, although she was the county assistant district attorney in Pinecrest, Oklahoma.

Gabriel said nothing as he passed her and headed for the checkout.

Her throat burning, Kira stared at his broad back, his narrow waist, his long legs that went well with his six-and-a-half foot frame. The black T-shirt he wore even though it was December revealed his muscular arms and build. In the years she'd known him, he'd never been bothered by the cold whereas she hated winter and its bleakness. He seemed to thrive in it.

Her legs buckled. Her grip on the cart tightened while she sucked in deep breaths to calm the thundering beat of her heart.

"Why, Gabriel, it's good to see you're back," the woman at the checkout counter said while ringing up his three items.

"Thanks, Mary Lou. That's the friendliest welcome I've gotten since I returned a few days ago."

"Well, you know how some people in this town can be."

Gabriel pocketed his change. "So true."

"I knew you could never have done those awful things they accused you of." Mary Lou hunched her shoulders as though a blast of cold swept into the grocery store. "But to think the person responsible is still out there." She waved her hand toward the street." I never used to lock my doors at night, but I bought deadbolts for all my doors when those three bodies were found. And I still don't feel safe."

"I'm sure he'll be caught soon. We have such a good police force in Pinecrest." He slid his sharp, accusing look toward Kira.

She still stood a few feet from the checkout aisle, not having moved a foot since she'd seen him. He let his gaze travel down her length inch by slow inch before it came back to rest on her face, trapping her as if he had the ability to paralyze her. She tried to muster her anger at his intimidating techniques, but she couldn't. She was responsible for putting him falsely in prison for eight months.

"Don't be a stranger." Mary Lou smiled, two dimples appearing.

Gabriel took the plastic bag from Mary Lou. "I'm not going anywhere. Pinecrest is my home."

Kira shivered. The words sounded like a threat directed at her.

He tipped his black cowboy hat at Mary Lou then turned his full attention on Kira. "Afternoon, Miss Davis." He nodded toward her, sending her a long look as hot and edgy as a western Oklahoma summer.

He walked from the grocery store and climbed into his black pickup, his stride belying the leashed power beneath the surface.

He had a right to hate her. She'd gone after him with a vengeance at the murder trial of her best friend, Marcie. At the time, she'd thought it justified vengeance.

Kira finally steered her cart to the checkout aisle and began placing her groceries on the conveyor belt. She'd only been doing her job, prosecuting Gabriel Michaels for second-degree murder. But seeing him, knowing he had just been released from prison, brought all the guilt she'd felt to the foreground. Two more women who'd gone missing during Gabriel's incarceration were found buried in separate graves alongside Marcie with the accompanying note: *Stop me.*

"Paper or plastic?"

Kira blinked. "What?"

"Do you want paper or plastic for your groceries?"

"I guess—paper, please." Kira tried to ignore the tightness in Mary Lou's voice, but it was hard to overlook the narrowed eyes, the tense mouth set in a frown.

"I don't know how you sleep at night, Kira Davis. First, you convict the wrong man. You take him away from his daughter. And now, a maniac is running around murdering women and taunting you. It's not right! You should have prosecuted the right person last spring for Marcie's murder. Shirley and Rebecca would be alive today."

In the background, Christmas music played over the PA system, making a mockery of the exchange. There was nothing peaceful and uplifting about being hated by certain people in town while a madman continued to terrorize it.

A dull ache behind Kira's eyes throbbed. The muscles in her neck grew taut and hard. "The police are doing their best."

Mary Lou snorted. "Well, that ain't good enough. Thankfully, at least Gabriel was in prison when the other murders occurred, or I'm sure you would have arrested him for those deaths, too." The cashier sacked the groceries with no regard to how she placed them in the paper bag.

Kira closed her eyes, hoping that would quiet the pounding against her skull. It didn't. Pinecrest, the county seat, was a nice, peaceful town of twenty thousand. Murder and rape weren't supposed to happen here. But they had—three times in the past eleven months.

"That'll be fifty-two dollars and twenty-three cents."

Wanting to escape Mary Lou's wrath, Kira quickly swiped her credit card and signed in the little black box. As she walked away, Kira realized it would be hard to escape something she felt each waking moment since the nightmare began almost a year ago with Marcie's disappearance. Remembering the sight of what had to be the murder scene nauseated her then and now. Blood everywhere. Although there wasn't a body, the blood was her best friend's and the medical examiner ruled there was no way she could have survived.

Until a few weeks ago, uncertainty plagued her when she remembered how Gabriel looked at her in the courtroom. Now there was no doubt. He'd been innocent in spite of the phone call from Marcie about Gabriel coming after her. Then there was Marcie's blood on his shirt and in the sink as though he tried to clean up before taking Marcie from her house.

When Kira left the grocery store, she surveyed the main street that ran through Pinecrest, studying the people around her as if that would help discern who was really responsible for murdering three women. She and the police had already made one mistake and sent the wrong man to prison. She couldn't afford to make that kind of mistake again. It cost two additional women their lives since Marcie's disappearance/murder. Their deaths were on her conscience, and no amount of reasoning on her part could change the fact she felt responsible for the present situation.

She placed the three grocery bags on the front seat of her Chevy then rounded the hood and slipped behind the steering wheel. The tension produced with Gabriel's return dug deep. She'd heard three days earlier he was back. She'd hoped to avoid him because she didn't know what to say. She usually never ran from a difficult situation, but what could she say to the innocent man she'd sent to prison?

Is I'm sorry enough?

Kira pulled into the steady stream of five o'clock traffic and headed home. All she wanted to do was soak in a hot bath and try washing away her worries. Of course, nothing she did would alter what was happening in Pinecrest now. That was the worst part, the hopelessness she felt in the face of this madman who lived to taunt her and the police with their mistakes.

When she turned down her street, her grandmother's old Cadillac sat at the curb. She groaned, knowing the hot bath would have to wait. After a frustrating day in court, she wasn't sure she could handle a frustrating conversation with Grams, whose one goal in life was to see her granddaughter married and pregnant.

Kira was lifting the groceries from her front seat when Grams approached, taking one sack from her. By the determined look in her grandmother's eyes, she knew this would be a *long* evening.

"My dear, I hadn't heard from you in a couple of days, and I got worried."

"There's no need to worry, Grams."

"Worry! Child, there's a killer running around Pinecrest, murdering beautiful girls. You fall into that category. I wish you would move in with me until this—this lunatic is caught."

"We'd cramp each other's style."

"In other words, you like your freedom. No ties. No commitments."

Every conversation in the past couple of years with her grandmother had always come around to the subject of marriage. Kira sighed and shifted the bags so she could open the front door. "One disastrous marriage was enough for me. I don't hate men, Grams. I just don't want to get tied down to one again." Kira set the two bags on the kitchen counter and started putting her groceries away. "Can't you just accept that and move on?"

"No, child. I'm not giving up on you even if you have on yourself. Somewhere there's a man who's perfect for you." She patted her chest over her heart. "I know it in here."

"My soul mate?" Kira couldn't contain her laugh. Ever since she could remember, her grandmother had filled her head with notions that there was one man in this world who was Kira's other half. Grams had found such a man, and she thought everyone else could, too. It didn't put her grandmother off that her own daughter had been married three times and was working on her fourth.

"Don't be so cynical. Jonathan wasn't that man. I told you that when you married him."

"Yeah, *after* the wedding. That was a little late." But even if her grandmother had said anything before the wedding, that wouldn't have stopped her from marrying Jonathan Bennett. She had thought herself deeply in love until he'd hit her.

"I couldn't say anything because y'all eloped, and I didn't really know the young man until later." Her grandmother opened the refrigerator door and slipped in the quart of milk. "At least one good thing came out of your split-up."

Kira stiffened, memories of the ugly divorce, the trauma she had endured, sweeping through her mind like a sandstorm. She couldn't imagine anything good coming from her failed marriage.

"Child, don't look at me as if I've grown two heads. You finally came home. I call that a good thing even if you don't."

"Home is good," Kira murmured then remembered the women's mutilated bodies the police found several weeks ago.

"You left Pinecrest so fast after you graduated from high school that I think my head actually spun."

The visual image of her grandmother's head spinning brought a short laugh to Kira. "Nothing rattles you, Grams."

"You're a pretty tough cookie yourself."

"Not as tough as I would like."

"What's bothering you? The murders?"

Kira finished placing the canned goods in the cabinet and closed the door. She faced her grandmother. "Yes—no."

"Which is it?"

"The *it* is a man. Gabriel Michaels to be exact. I saw him today."

"Oh my, child, that might rattle even me. What did he say to you?"

"'Afternoon, Miss Davis.'"

"That's all?"

"He didn't have to say anything else. He said it all with his eyes." *The most compelling gray eyes.* Kira recalled how he had looked so intently, heatedly at her in the grocery store. Just the remembrance brought a tightening in her stomach.

"If my memory serves me right, he's one handsome fella."

"Your memory is as sharp as ever. Nothing much gets by you."

"Have you told the man you're sorry?"

"I was doing my job." Her legs suddenly giving out on her, Kira sat at the kitchen table. The day had been too long and tension-filled.

Her grandmother took the chair opposite Kira. "True. But maybe that boy needs to hear from you. I imagine that whole affair nearly destroyed his life."

"I wouldn't know where to begin."

"How about with I'm sorry? Nothing fancy. Keep it simple."

"Grams, life isn't simple."

"Sure it is. You're born. You live. You die. Nothing's simpler than that. He may need to hear the words from you, but more importantly, I think you need to say those words to him. Ever since the bodies were found, you've been beating yourself up over this whole affair. Go to him. Tell him you're sorry."

The thought of facing Gabriel Michaels made Kira's heart slow to a painful throb. Beads of sweat popped out on her forehead. She swiped them away with a shaky hand. She'd never been a coward—until now. "I guess I could go see him at his ranch tomorrow."

* * *

Gabriel sat at his office desk at his ranch, staring out the window at the landscape some would say was almost barren, bleak. But he felt a kinship with this semi-arid land, an appreciation for its raw beauty. He was home and didn't ever intend to leave again.

Thank You, Lord, for freeing me from prison.

He closed his eyes and tried to focus on the present. Christmas would be in three weeks. He'd be here to enjoy it with his eight-year-old daughter, Abbey, and his sister, Jessie, not in...Memories of the past months threatened what little peace he had achieved since coming home. He'd been doing fine until he saw Kira Davis yesterday at the grocery store.

They had known each other for years, especially after he married her best friend. But when it came to believing him about his wife's disappearance, she couldn't. Yes, he had Marcie's blood on his shirt because she came at him with a knife. He finally managed to wrestle it away but not before he was cut in several places in the struggle. They had been in the kitchen. He quickly washed his hands and wrapped one in a towel.

When Marcie turned toward him, she was on her cell. He'd intended to leave until she settled down, but then he saw her bleeding palm, blood dripping from it. He wanted to check it because she'd been drinking, but she screamed and attacked him again, her long fingernails gouging his upper arm, ripping his T-shirt. He hurried from the place with her yelling obscenities. She was very much alive when he pulled away from the house she'd lived in since their separation. And he didn't come back a couple of hours later, as the police thought, and kill his wife then get rid of her body.

Not when his daughter was at the ranch. She'd been crying because her mommy had called and postponed their time together for a couple of days—again. He hated seeing Abbey so upset. He needed to make Marcie realize what cancelling repeatedly was doing to their daughter. But what occurred later was far worse.

Gabriel shook those memories away, determined to put the past behind him. He had too much that demanded his attention now to focus any more energy on what had happened. His daughter needed him more than ever. His ranch did, too. Jessie and Hank, his cowhand, had tried to keep things going, but his absence had taken a toll on their income.

As he rose, an image of a tall woman with long blond hair that hung about her shoulders in thick waves and blue eyes that were stabbing in their assessment of him flooded his mind. He tensed, his hands balling at his sides. Kira Davis, the county assistant DA responsible for sending him to prison, should have at least listened to his story.

He thought of all that had happened since his conviction, and he couldn't contain his anger. It bolted through him as swift as lightning. Seeing the cell door slam on him had killed his mother from a broken heart. Now he was fighting to retain full custody of his own daughter from her grandmother, Ruth Morgan, a powerful woman who had all the time and money to spend on her fight to save her only granddaughter from a nightmarish fate, as she had called living with him.

Gabriel picked up the legal documents announcing Ruth's intention to seek at least partial custody of Abbey. He crushed them in his hand, tossing them into the trashcan. He wished he could rid himself of the problem as easily as throwing the papers away. But the next few months would be even worse than the previous ones. Abbey was his daughter, and no one was going to take her away from him even if he had to sell his ranch to fight this in court.

No one.

The sound of a car approaching drew Gabriel's attention back to the window. As Kira climbed from her Chevy, scanned the yard, then walked toward the porch, he froze. She was all legs, which were emphasized by her short black skirt. In spite of his anger at her, Gabriel admired the way the woman carried herself, proud with an almost defiant attitude.

Why is she here? Hadn't she done enough?

He pushed himself away from the desk and headed toward the front door. Wanting to throw her off guard as much as possible, he opened it before she had a chance to knock. She dropped her hand to her side and faced him with the screen door the only thing that separated them—that and the fact this woman was one of the reasons his life had fallen apart.

"Lost?" he drawled, leaning against the doorjamb as though he had not a care in the world while inside he was wound so tight he wondered if he would explode right before her eyes. "The main highway is that way." He nodded toward the north.

"I came to see you."

He heard the trace of unease in her voice, and for some reason that bothered him. "I couldn't have killed the other two women. Thankfully, I have the perfect alibi. I was in prison at the time those murders were committed."

"May I come in?"

He didn't want her in his house, invading his sanctuary, disturbing his daughter. He opened the screen door and stepped out onto the porch. "What do you want?"

Her gaze that had been on him the whole time slid away, panned the yard as if she was looking for a way to escape. She swallowed hard. "I came to apologize for"— she faltered, swallowing again—"I'm sorry for everything."

"Fine. I'm sure you feel better. You've done what you came here to do, so now you can leave."

She looked him in the eye. "I was doing my job. It wasn't personal."

"Ma'am, from where I was sitting in the

courtroom, it was very personal. You were Marcie's best friend. You, along with her esteemed family, didn't approve of her marrying below her station, as they told me on more than one occasion. It wasn't enough that we were getting divorced. No, it was important that y'all pin the assault and supposed murder on me even though I had an alibi."

"Your mother was considered bias."

"I couldn't change who I was with at the time of the assault to have a more impartial alibi. If I'd known I needed one, I would have stood in the middle of Main Street and caused a scene so people would remember me."

A flush stained her cheeks. "I'm sorry about your mother."

"That she died? Or that she had to see her only son dragged away to prison for a crime he didn't commit?"

She flinched. "Both."

He had to give her credit for having guts. Most people wouldn't have set foot on his ranch after what she'd done. But here she was, standing in front of him with the sun quickly sinking below the flat horizon as she offered him an apology. "Well, as you said, it was your job." He turned toward the door, wanting to end the conversation as quickly as possible.

"Please, don't go yet."

The plea in her voice touched his hardened heart, and he hesitated, his back to her, his hand on the door handle. God wanted him to forgive her for the past, but he didn't know if he could.

"I need your help."

He pivoted, bringing him only a foot from her. He could smell her scent of lilacs and was momentarily taken back. He was reminded of softness and a warm spring day, like the day he'd been hauled off to prison. Clamping down his jaw to keep his temper in control, he stared at her, swallowing the words, "Have you gone mad?"

"I'll understand if you don't want to help me, but you knew Marcie better than anyone. You were married to her for eight years. Maybe you know something that could help us find the man committing these crimes."

He threw back his head and laughed, not even remotely humorous. "Now, y'all want to know what I know. Don't you think it's eleven months too late?"

"It's never too late to help."

He thrust his face into hers, relishing the fear that leaped into her eyes. "Lady, get off my property. I don't owe you or anyone in Pinecrest a thing."

"But—"

He slammed into the house and struck the doorjamb with his fist, welcoming the pain that shot up his arm. His anger shook him to his core. He sucked in deep breaths to rein in his rage. Abbey was in the kitchen with his sister. He wouldn't allow this whole ugly affair to touch her any more than it already had. He had to protect his daughter.

"Daddy, is someone here? I heard voices." His daughter came from the back of the house, her forehead furrowed.

"It was no one, princess." He walked to her and tousled her blond hair. When she looked up at him, his heart seemed to stop beating for a second. She was an exact replica of her mother.

"I finished my homework. Jessie and me are gonna fix dinner. What do you want?"

"Surprise me, honey."

"Ah, Daddy, you always say that."

"I like surprises."

"No, you don't."

"Okay, maybe only ones from you."

Abbey threw her arms around his waist and hugged him. "I love you. We'll make something special. One of your favorites."

As his daughter skipped into the kitchen, his throat thickened. His eyes blurred. He closed them, continuing to inhale calming breaths until his ironclad control fell back into place. He still saw the fear in her eyes. She was scared he would go away again. She was trying to be brave, but she had hardly let him out of her sight when she wasn't at school. The Lord and thoughts of Abbey were the reason he had kept his sanity in prison. No one would ever take her away from him again, especially her grandmother. He had promised Abbey that the day he'd returned home, and he would keep that promise no matter what.

* * *

What had she expected? The welcome wagon? Kira stared at the closed door, fighting the urge to pound on it in frustration.

Whatever had possessed her to apologize one minute and ask for his help the next? Desperation. She pivoted and stalked to her car. When she'd come out to the ranch, she hadn't intended to ask for his help. But after it slipped out, gaining Gabriel's help in the search for the murderer made a lot of sense. He knew Marcie better than she had because until two years ago she'd lived in Tulsa where she'd gone to college then become an assistant district attorney. She'd been away from Pinecrest except for an occasional visit for over nine years.

Definitely, she was desperate—and frightened—at what was happening in town. The police chief would tell her that very thing when she told him what she had in mind. They needed anyone and everyone's help—even Gabriel—to find this killer before he took another life. She couldn't shake the feeling the last two women's deaths were her fault. If only she and the police had dug deeper into Marcie's disappearance last January. They should have investigated all the possibilities as Gabriel had urged. But they had circumstantial and forensic evidence placing him at the scene of the crime. No one lost that much blood and didn't die. If only they had accepted his alibi and looked at other possible perpetrators.

Kira shuddered. These regrets would get her nowhere. She would have to go home and start over, reviewing everything that had been gathered at the crime scenes and the place where the murderer buried the three women. There was a clue somewhere in all those pages of collected evidence. She had to find it before someone else died. It wasn't her job to investigate, but this time when they arrested the killer, she wanted no doubt of his guilt.

She yanked open her car door and climbed inside then glanced once more at Gabriel's one story adobe style house. How could she get the man to help? She could send the police to question him again about Marcie, but she knew instinctively that would only encourage his silence. He might hate her, but his feelings toward the police in Pinecrest ran even deeper. Marcie's family had a lot of pull in the town, practically owning half of it and, no doubt, they were behind Gabriel's quick arrest and trial. And she hadn't protested at the time.

A knot of tension in her neck spread through her shoulders. She rolled her head, massaging the tautness, but nothing she did alleviated the pain. Starting the car, she decided she would try again in a day or so. She needed Gabriel's input about Marcie's actions those last years.

She wouldn't wait long, though, because she had a gut feeling that the murderer would kill again. Soon. The second and third disappearances were only ten weeks apart while he'd waited six months after Marcie's. With each corpse, he left a note with *stop me* stuffed into their mouths. And short of being caught, more women would be murdered. He wasn't through.

Cranking her window down a few inches, Kira aimed her car down the graded dirt drive. She saw Gabriel's ranch as if for the first time. The vastness. The absolute isolation. Burnt orange, umber, and sienna streaked the darkening sky, lending eeriness to the already lonely scene. The high thin clouds resembled a demon's long, slender fingers stirring the evil already pulsating in the town's air.

Eager to slip out of her pensive mood and into the hot bath she'd been craving, Kira nudged her foot a little harder on the gas, relieved when about a quarter mile up the road, she caught sight of the ranch's main gate.

Pop!

Her car lurched to the right. A blow out? The noise came again, sounding more like firecrackers than a blown tire. She slammed on the brakes.

Pop. Pop. Pop, pop, pop.

Struggling to compensate for the car's violent right pull, she steered hard to the left while pumping the brakes. But it was no use. The Chevy had started a slow spin on the bone-dry dirt. Already, the front wheels—or what was left of them—pointed in a sickening yaw toward the deep ditch lining the road.

I forgot to put on my seatbelt.

With no time for that, she braced herself for the impact. Crashing into the ditch pitched her forward, smashing her forehead into the steering wheel then whipping her neck back. At a sixty-degree angle, she fell against the steering wheel. Blackness swirled about the edges of her mind as she tried to lift her head. Pain streaked down her neck.

She moaned and rested her cheek against the cold plastic she was still gripping so tightly her hands felt numb.

The dark void edged closer. She fought to stay alert. Something wasn't right.

Someone shot at me.

TWO

Gabriel stood in the kitchen doorway watching Abbey help Jessie fix dinner. He had a lot of work to do, but he couldn't seem to see enough of his daughter. He was as bad as she about not being far from one another for too long.

When he'd gone to prison, he'd thought he would never see her again. Marcie's mother swooped in and took Abbey to live with her. She began seeking full custody of his daughter. With Ruth's connections in town and the state, his mother and Jessie didn't have a choice. Ruth Morgan, his daughter's grandmother, wouldn't even let Abbey come to see him when Jessie did, and with his finances exhausted completely because of his trial, he didn't have the money to fight Ruth in court. Ultimately, he didn't even try because he hadn't wanted his daughter to see him like that. Nor had he wanted Abbey dragged through a court battle and forced to choose between her grandmother Morgan and his sister. At least, he'd been able to talk to her once a week on the phone, but that hadn't been enough. Later, when new evidence came forward to free him, the court terminated Ruth's request for full custody.

But when he returned to Pinecrest, Ruth had to bring his daughter back to the ranch. The next day, Ruth filed for partial custody.

Sitting in his cell, he'd thought of what he would miss in Abbey's life: her first date, her high school graduation, her wedding. That realization nearly killed him more than dealing with the lowlifes in prison, more than knowing he was innocent and not able to prove it.

Those feeling of hopelessness swamped him anew. His throat closed. He'd promised himself he wouldn't go back to that place in his mind. In prison, he'd fought it and hung onto his faith. He had to believe the Lord was with him every step of the way.

Abbey giggled at something Jessie said, looked back at him, and grinned then resumed working on the salad.

The sound of her laughter nearly choked him. He gritted his teeth and turned into the dining room. Walking through it, he crossed his living room to the large window and stared at the road and Kira's Chevy. It crested an incline not far from the highway and disappeared from view.

He started to turn away when a sound like a car backfiring resonated in the air. Then similar noises followed.

Gunshots?

Gabriel whipped around, snatched his rifle and a box of ammunition from the closet, and raced for the front door. "Jessie, Abbey, stay in the house," he shouted over his shoulder as he hurried outside into the gray light of early evening.

More rapid-fire pops punctured the twilight quiet. Gabriel slowed only long enough to load his rifle then ran down his dirt road toward the highway.

Was Kira in trouble?

He came to a stop at the top of the rise, his rifle clutched in his hands. The rear end of the Chevy stuck up in a ditch. Although quiet now, there was no way her car backfired that many times. Before charging down the incline, he scanned the terrain. Multiple hiding places taunted him. What if she was hurt?

Lord, protect me.

With his gun raised, he hurried toward the wreck. His heart hammered against his rib cage as he rushed to the car, one part of him acknowledging the foolishness of exposing himself to a shooter. But the other part couldn't have stopped if he'd wanted. This was his land, and no one was going to hurt anyone while he was around. Not even Kira Davis.

"Are you okay?" he yelled as he slid a few feet down into the ditch, his pulse rapid, his breathing shallow.

* * *

Through the foggy haze, Kira heard the question and started to answer. Then she realized who had asked it, and for once, she couldn't speak. The one person who had more reason than most to shoot at her inquired if she was all right.

Lifting her throbbing head from the steering wheel, she fumbled for her black purse and the gun she kept inside. The sudden movement caused her world to tilt then spin. She closed her eyes for a second then tried to focus on the interior of the car, but the shadows of night were creeping closer. She couldn't see her handbag on the passenger seat. She squinted at the floorboard in case it was thrown off in the crash. Still too dark. Panic gripped her.

Could Gabriel have shot at her car?

"Kira."

His voice was nearer. This time she heard the concern in it and tried to think what to do. Her mind couldn't latch onto a string of words to say. She sank back against the seat, briefly wondering why her airbag hadn't deployed. Thinking took too much energy. All she wanted to do was close her eyes and go to sleep. Maybe then she would awaken in her own bed, safe, alone, all the nightmares of the past few weeks gone.

But Gabriel's face appeared at her driver's side window, his harsh lines cut into a frown of anger—or was it worry? She raised her hand to her temple to massage the spot above her right eye where it hurt. When she touched the area, pain lanced through her. As she sucked in a gulp of air, she pulled her fingers away. A sticky wetness covered them, the scent of blood wafting to her.

"Kira, are you all right?"

That was concern. He wasn't going to kill her. She attempted a smile that she knew faded instantly. She sank against the steering wheel, the effort to hold herself upright too much. "Glad you're here," she murmured, her eyes closing halfway.

Gabriel wrenched the door open and checked her head, his fingertips grazing her cheeks, forehead. "I'll have to go back to the house to call for an ambulance."

"No. Don't. Someone was shooting at me." Her gaze latched onto the rifle slung over his shoulder. She tried to scramble away.

He clasped her arm and stilled her movement. "I don't want to move you in case—"

"Did you?" She stared at his hand on her.

He scowled. "What? Shoot at you? If I had, I wouldn't be here."

"But why are you here?"

"You're in trouble. I heard the shots from my house."

She sagged back. The effort of tensing along with the elephants stampeding inside her head hurt.

"Sit still. Let me check to see if anything is wrong besides the cut over your eye." He tunneled his hand into her hair, pressing gently to feel for any other injuries. "Where do you hurt?"

"My head mostly. I think I can get out. No ambulance."

He continued his inspection, his fingers

lightly moving along the column of her neck. "I have a feeling that'll hurt later." He peered down. "You weren't wearing your seatbelt."

"My thoughts were preoccupied. Why didn't the airbag deploy, though?"

"The sensors weren't triggered because of your speed or braking most likely."

When he straightened, his arms falling to his sides, she sighed with relief. His gentle touch sent her pulse racing. Her stomach knotted at his nearness, not because she was afraid. No, it was worse. Her body reacted as if she was attracted to him.

"I expect you'll feel more than a headache tomorrow morning."

She carefully swung her legs around in preparation of moving from her car. She needed space between them. She was going to stand on her own. Her mind still focused on the feel of his hands on her. "I'm fine. Just a little shaken."

One of Gabriel's eyebrows lifted. "Just a little? Someone was shooting at you." He gestured toward the front of the Chevy.

"There are a few bullet holes to prove it."

She started to rise, but weakness attacked her legs. Sitting again, she gripped the steering wheel and seat to give it another try.

"Here. At least let me help you out of the car."

"No, really. I'm fine." She closed her eyes to gather what energy she needed.

He muttered something about stubborn women and reached inside to assist her from the car whether she wanted it or not. His arms supported most of her weight as she slipped from the front seat. He brought her flat against him, her hands on his shoulders.

When she looked up at him, the car's interior light accentuated the hard planes of his face. She wanted to step away, but she felt trapped by his smoldering look. With a hard shake of his head, he moved back although his hands still rested at her waist. Intensity poured from him. It went under her skin as if he were probing deep into her soul for answers. She wasn't sure she wanted him to read her that intimately, for anyone to get that close to her ever again.

Finally, he glanced away. "I'll help you back to the house where you can call for assistance with your car. Then I'm taking you to the hospital."

"I don't think—"

"This is not up for negotiation. You need to see a doctor. You probably have a concussion. Let's go." He slid his arm around her again to help her up the incline.

Remembering why she was in this situation in the first place, Kira pulled away. "I need to check something. I want to take a look at the damage to my car before it's completely dark."

"You wait here. I'll take a look. You don't need to move around anymore than necessary."

"Did anyone ever tell you that you're bossy?"

Ignoring her question, he circled her Chevy, pausing a few places to inspect closer in the dim light from the car. "Someone besides me doesn't like what you do for a living." He came to her, dusting off his jeans where he'd knelt.

"Have you made anyone angry lately?"

"Besides you? My job is to prosecute criminals."

"And innocent people," he muttered until his breath.

But she heard it. "I work hard not to do that."

"Obviously not hard enough."

"Until recently Pinecrest has been a quiet town with the occasional drunk driver, assault, burglary."

"But not murder."

"You know as well as I do the last one was four years ago and that was an easy case for the county assistant DA. Keith Johnson shot his wife in front of about half a dozen people at his New Year's Eve party. This situation is much different." The thought that an unknown assailant was using her for target practice unnerved her more than she wanted to acknowledge. The peaceful hometown she'd returned to was no longer the haven she had been seeking.

She was caught in a nightmare, playing the starring role with no idea what the script would require her to do next. The myriad possibilities chilled her, further fueled by the darkness that had completely settled over the terrain.

Is the shooter still out there watching us?

"Let's get back to the house. I'm sure the gunman is gone by now, but I don't want to take any chances." He reached in and switched off her headlights then shut the door.

"You'll get no argument from me."

Again he wrapped his arm about her to support her while they climbed out of the ditch. On the walk back to his house, Kira's knees wobbled and walking in a straight line proved impossible. She clung to Gabriel's side, afraid that she would collapse at his feet. Now that would be a sight he'd probably like to see—her at his feet, helpless. She chuckled at the thought.

"I'm glad you can laugh about what happened."

"I think shock is setting in."

"Cold?"

Far from it. The night temperature was dropping fast, and she should be cold with only a long sleeve blouse to protect her. "No, I feel…unsteady."

That was a good word to describe what she was experiencing. He would chalk it up to the accident, which was partially true, but also his presence disturbed her, not because he was responsible for shooting her car but because he was a dangerous man—ruthless, relentless, and if Marcie were right, unforgiving.

He nestled her more firmly against his side, which sent her pulse rate rocketing. She tried to concentrate on all the stories Marcie told her about her husband when they were going through their divorce, but she couldn't remember any. All she thought about was he'd come out to check on her when he'd heard the gunshots. The man Marcie described would never have done that.

At Gabriel's house, he unlocked his front door and let Kira enter first. The scent of onions sautéing on the stove filled her nostrils. When he relocked the door, what had happened to her was reinforced, along with the fact that he thought the person could still be outside. She hugged her arms to ward off the sudden coldness now sweeping through her.

"You can make your calls in my office." He walked to a room at the right of the entrance hall. Inside, he indicated the phone on his desk. "I'll be back in a minute."

Kira waited until he left before sinking down onto the chair he sat in while working. Her hand trembled as she picked up the receiver and placed her first call to her automobile club. Then she made a second one to the police chief. The dispatcher put her call through to Chief Bill Shaffer in his car.

"This is Kira. I've had a problem I need you to check into. I'm at the Michaels' ranch—"

The police chief swore. "What are you doing there? Are you all right? If that—"

"Bill, I'm fine," she cut him off before he began ranting about Gabriel. "My car was shot at a few minutes ago when I was leaving the ranch. Gabriel wasn't responsible."

"How do you know? Did you see who it was?"

"No, but I know he didn't," she said with a conviction she truly felt. "Gabriel helped me back to his house. A couple of my tires are ruined, along with several bullet holes in the side of my car. He risked his own life to come see if I was all right."

"If you didn't see who did the shooting, then how do you really know?"

How do I? She thought back over the past thirty minutes and realized how. "The shots came from the highway. He couldn't be in two places at once. I know this is out of your jurisdiction, but please check into it for me, and Bill," she paused and took a deep breath, "please don't accuse him of anything. We've put him through enough."

"We followed the leads we had at the time. We didn't do anything wrong."

And if Bill had his way, Gabriel would still be in prison. Marcie played on the fact Bill had a crush on her, and she used to wrap him around her little finger. "We put the wrong man behind bars. I don't call that right. I'll be at the hospital if you need me."

"I thought you told me that everything was all right."

She released a long sigh. "Gabriel insists I see a doctor. I hit my head on the steering wheel. I have the beginnings of a bump that'll probably rival Mount Everest before it's over with." She closed her eyes because the pounding behind them was intensifying, and she really did believe that shock was finally setting in. Goosebumps covered her from head to toe. She could have been seriously injured or dead. One shudder after another rippled through her.

"I'll let you know what I find, Kira. Probably nothing much before morning."

"Thanks." When she hung up, she swiveled around to find Gabriel leaning against the doorjamb watching her. Warmth crept up her face. "Do you eavesdrop often?"

"Only when I'm the subject of the conversation." He pushed away. "Are you ready to go?"

Weariness blanketed her. The aches and bruises were starting to emerge. She wished she could talk him into taking her home. But he was probably right about seeing a doctor. That didn't mean she had to like it. "Yes."

"My daughter and sister will ride with us."

"Don't trust yourself to be alone with me?"

"You never know when you'll need an alibi that can stand up in court. Of course, my sister's and daughter's would be considered biased according to you and the police."

She started to tell him she was sorry again but realized they were only words, which wouldn't mean anything to him. She figured the only way he would really forgive her was if she could miraculously give him back the past months of his life as a free man. She couldn't, so she would have to live with the fact that this man wouldn't forgive her or ever trust her. There was a part of her that didn't blame him. She certainly had no intention of forgiving Jonathan for what *he'd* done to her.

As she passed Gabriel to go into the

hallway, he murmured, "Neither Jessie nor Abbey know anything about someone shooting at you. I told them your car backfired and you wrecked it. I would like it to remain that way. They don't need to be frightened any more than they already are with the events of the past few weeks."

She heard the protective ring to his voice and nodded.

"If I could leave them here, I would."

"But they aren't safe?"

"Safe? No one in Pinecrest is right now."

"You think it's the murderer who shot at me?"

"Maybe. Either way I intend to find the person responsible."

The steel thread that ran through his declaration underlined the element of danger Kira sensed surrounding Gabriel. He was very capable of carrying out any threat he made. In this instant, she understood how he felt. His home and family were being threatened, and he wouldn't stand by idly and let that happen.

"You can't take the law into your own hands." She didn't want anything else to go wrong for him.

"The gunman made a big mistake when he trespassed on my land," Gabriel whispered, looking beyond Kira. An iron determination glinted in his eyes.

She turned.

Abbey stood next to Jessie. Gabriel's sister didn't look anything like him. Petite, she had long blond hair and blue eyes. Right now those eyes were conveying a message of hatred, directed at her.

"Kira!" Abbey grinned.

She offered the eight-year-old a smile, aware of Abbey's father behind Kira, alert, ready to pounce if she said or did anything to alarm his daughter. "Hi. I haven't seen you in a while." Every time she saw Marcie's daughter, she couldn't help but think about her friend. They looked so much alike.

"Daddy told me you had an accident." Abbey approached Kira, a tiny frown lining her brow as she stared at Kira's forehead and handed her a plastic bag with ice. "Maybe this will help. Aunt Jessie fixed it for you."

Kira took it from Abbey. "Thanks. I'm sure it will, honey."

"We're taking you to the hospital," Abbey said in a serious voice, her gaze glued to Kira's forehead.

She waved her hand as though to dismiss the bump that was probably growing before their very eyes. "This is nothing, but I should get it checked out to be on the safe side. I'm glad you're going to ride with us. I haven't seen you in a while."

"I've been at my grandmother's house until lately."

Which was a fortress. If only Marcie had been living with her mother, a matriarch of a powerful, wealthy family, and not in one of the houses her mother rented out, she might not have died. But Marcie had hated being at the estate and had wanted her freedom from her controlling mom—had all her life.

Tension radiated from Gabriel, and he reached out and gripped Kira.

She glanced at his hand on her arm as though he often touched her. She didn't want Abbey to sense any tension from her toward her father. "I hope you'll fill me in on how school's going for you. I hear you have Mrs. Carter. I had her when I was in elementary school."

"Yeah, she's ancient."

Kira smiled at the comment. Mrs. Carter was probably forty-five years old and wouldn't appreciate being called that. "I can remember having tons of homework."

"Spelling, math, and reading every night," Abbey said with a moan then followed her father out onto the front porch. "But Daddy and Jessie help me with it." The little girl took Gabriel's hand while he slung an arm over Kira's shoulder as they all walked to his black F-150 parked at the side of the house.

Trying to ignore his closeness, Kira searched for something to say. "You're lucky, Abbey. I didn't have anyone to help me." She slid a glance toward Gabriel and his daughter and envied their close relationship. She'd never known her father, and her mother had been too busy with the men in her life to sit down and help her with anything.

"What about your mother or father?" Abbey asked while she and Jessie climbed into the backseat of the pickup.

After Kira slipped into the front with Gabriel's help, he rounded the hood, climbed into the driver's seat, and switched on the engine. She wasn't sure how to answer the girl. Kira saw the white-knuckled grip Gabriel had on the steering wheel and realized the subject was an uncomfortable one for him. He was being very protective of his daughter where her mother was concerned, but he wouldn't be able to shield her for long. Life had a way of intruding when least expected. "Once my mom hired a math tutor, but that was all. And my grams was always supportive." The second she mentioned her grandmother thunder descended over his features. Abbey's grandmother was a force to be reckoned with, and no doubt, she'd made Gabriel's life miserable. Few people went up against the woman, but he had when he'd married Marcie.

He headed for the highway. "Speaking

of homework, sweetheart, did you get your spelling sentences done and that page of math?"

Silence greeted his question.

He glanced at his daughter then his sister. "I gather that's a no."

"Daddy, I was going to after dinner."

"Now, you're going to when we get home."

Kira tensed the nearer they came to her wrecked car. Suddenly she remembered she didn't have her purse. "Stop!"

He slammed on the brakes. "What's wrong?"

"My purse is in the car. I need it." Kira started to open the door.

Gabriel mumbled something under his breath. "I'd better get it. There's a flashlight in the glove compartment."

She handed him the distinctly pink torch. He smirked before making his way to her car. In the darkness, she found it hard to tell what he was doing. The interior light came on when he opened the door, but still she couldn't see well because of the Chevy's angle in the ditch. She scanned the terrain, feeling as if someone were watching her like yesterday. The feeling crawled up her spine and sent goose bumps through her body.

Rubbing her hands up and down her arms, Kira twisted toward Abbey and Jessie. "When I came to your house, I smelled something cooking. Was that dinner?"

"Yes," Jessie said in a clipped voice. "We haven't eaten yet."

"I was helping Aunt Jessie make my daddy's favorite."

"What is it?" Kira asked, feeling the drill of Jessie's stare. Gabriel's sister's anger churned the air, and Kira was reminded again of yesterday in the grocery store when Mary Lou blamed her for what happened to Gabriel.

"Daddy loves spaghetti. Not out of a can but made from scratch. I chopped the green peppers for Aunt Jessie and was making the salad. She was making the sauce. She's a great cook."

"The extent of my cooking abilities is popping something in the microwave." Kira glanced out the window.

Gabriel climbed out of the ditch.

"Jessie, I'm sorry I interrupted dinner. Is it salvageable?"

"Yes," she answered as the door opened and the interior light illuminated the inside of the vehicle. Jessie's narrowed gaze and mouth firmed into a frown greeted Kira.

She wished she'd remained quiet earlier. There was no way Abbey didn't sense the hostility. She hoped the child thought her aunt was mad because of the interrupted dinner.

Gabriel climbed into the truck and tossed her purse to her. "It was on the floorboard."

"Thank you."

Kira gripped her black leather bag and tried to relax. She'd learned she couldn't change the past, and fretting over it wasn't worth the anguish. She could only influence what happened in the future, and she intended to make sure whoever was murdering these women would be brought to justice soon. Then maybe she could find some peace concerning Gabriel, Marcie, and the other two victims.

When they arrived in Pinecrest, Gabriel pulled up in front of Al's Diner. "Jessie, I want you and Abbey to get some dinner. I'm going to take Kira to the hospital then come back for y'all after I make sure everything is all right. Just wait inside for me."

"What are you gonna eat, Daddy?"

"I'll grab something. Don't you worry, princess. If I'm going to be longer than an hour, I'll call you."

Gabriel didn't leave until his daughter and sister were safely inside the diner. Then he backed out of the parking space and headed for the small hospital.

The tension in the pickup didn't dissipate with Jessie's exit. Kira's nerves were raw by the time they arrived at the emergency room entrance. The pounding in her head had increased, and her stomach roiled.

Gabriel assisted her from the truck. The movement awakened the aches caused by being tossed about. Again his arm went around her, and he supported some of her weight as they started for the entrance. With her headache so intense, the act of walking caused her world to spin. Inside he sat her in the first chair available and went up to the reception counter.

Kira rested her head back against the wall and closed her eyes, vaguely aware of the faint voices of Gabriel and the woman at the counter. But she knew the moment he was standing in front of her. She felt his presence deep inside and opened her eyes to stare up at him.

"They need your insurance card."

"Okay," she said slowly, trying to remember where she kept it. Everything was fuzzy. All she wanted to do was sleep.

"Is it in your purse?" Gabriel sat next to her.

"Yes." She clutched her purse in one hand and needed to pry her fingers loose.

"Do you want me to look for it?"

"No, I can." She straightened and opened her bag. Her eyes widened. Next to her gun and wallet was a scrap of paper— one she'd never seen before.

THREE

Kira's hand trembled as she gingerly pulled the yellowed scrap out of her purse. Bold letters cut from the newspaper, spelling, *stop me*, leaped off the page and struck her with their evil message. Stunned by the thought the murderer had been in her car only moments after she'd left it, she dropped the paper, the sheet floating to the emergency room floor.

Gabriel bent to pick up the paper.

"Don't!"

His gaze snapped back to hers.

"It's from him. The killer was in my car." She heard the hysterical tone in her voice but didn't care anymore if she presented a tough front. She wasn't tough. She wanted to cry. She wanted to be held. She wanted to run away and hide until it was safe.

Gabriel took one look at her face and tugged her into his arms. She nestled into his strength, unable to pull away. She didn't want to be alone, and for the first time, she had to admit she was afraid for the future, for Pinecrest, for herself. Tears glistened in her eyes, and she squeezed them shut, hoping she could hold herself together, not expose herself raw before this man who had every right to hate her.

"You need to call the police chief about the note." He stroked his hand down her back, his voice and touch gentle.

For a few seconds, all she could think about were his fingers moving down her spine. "This isn't the first one," she said finally and pulled away from the comfort of his embrace. "I got one at the office four weeks ago right before the third victim, Rebecca, disappeared."

"Do the police know?"

"Yes. Bill had his men all over the

courthouse five minutes after I notified him."

"Let me take a guess. No one saw anything."

"Not a thing. It's like the murderer can appear and disappear at will. Before the note, I received a phone call from him. He'd been upset about what he'd done to Marcie and Shirley. He told me specific details of the scene of Marcie's murder. Then he asked me to stop him. The call couldn't be traced, and his voice had been disguised."

"My lawyer told me even before the bodies were found the police had been looking at my case again. Is that why I was released so quickly after the women were discovered?"

"Yes. One of the details wasn't known to the public."

"A detail only the killer would have known..." Gabriel ran his fingers through his hair. "He took my freedom away and nearly cost me my daughter."

Kira stared up at him. "And his call also freed you. When the killer provided that information, I was sure you hadn't killed Marcie, and Ruth Morgan's fight for full custody of Abbey hinged on your guilt. I asked the court to delay the proceedings while we looked into the new piece of evidence."

The hard edge of Gabriel's expression attested to the intense emotions vying for dominance in him. "I owe you my freedom. What kind of game is he playing with you?"

"I'm starting to think he wants me to know he can get to me at any time. But then there are times I think he wants to be stopped."

"What's the police chief gonna do about it?"

"I carry a gun now." She opened her purse to show him. "Of course, it didn't do me much good this evening."

"Do you know how to use it?"

"Yes. Bill gave me lessons. His officers drive by my house at night, and at least once an evening, they ring the doorbell and check on me."

"You should have more protection than that, especially after what happened this evening."

"There aren't enough officers. Our resources are stretched thin just keeping up with this murderer, even with the sheriff's help."

"You still need to let the police chief know about this latest note. It seems like the killer is escalating. I'm gonna call Bill right now."

Wearily Kira rested her head against the wall again, exhaustion and the continuing hammering against her skull making her eyes droop and her stomach nauseated. "As I told you earlier, you don't have to. I will."

"Yes, I do."

The steel edge to his voice shouted she wouldn't be able to change his mind, and she didn't have it in her to argue.

Gabriel stood and walked to the counter, spoke to the receptionist, then took out his cell phone and placed a call. As the conversation progressed, his back tensed. Then his free hand ramrod straight at his side squeezed into a fist, and a scowl etched deeper into his features. There was definitely no love lost between Bill Shaffer and Gabriel Michaels. She wished she had the strength to make the call herself, but she found it difficult even to lift her arms.

After Gabriel finished talking on the phone, he spoke to the receptionist again. She came around the counter, retrieved a wheelchair, and rolled it to Kira.

"We'll get your information later. I hear you had a nasty ordeal this evening. Dr. Addison should be here shortly." The woman wheeled Kira to the second of the two examination rooms and glanced back at Gabriel. "Thank you. I've got it from here."

"Kira, I'll hang around for Chief Shaffer."

"You don't have to. I'll be all right here."

"It happened on my land. I'll wait."

"What about Jessie and Abbey?"

"I'll call them and let them know I'll be a little late. The police chief should be here soon."

* * *

Gabriel settled into a chair in the waiting room that gave him a view of the entrance to the exam room then took out his cell phone again and called his sister. "Jessie, I'll be later than I thought."

"Why are you staying at the hospital?" his sister asked. "Have you forgotten what that woman did to you?"

His grip on the phone tightened as he remembered the past months. "Not for one minute, but I want to see the police chief about what happened at the ranch this evening."

"What did happen? Why do you want to talk to him," she paused then whispered, "and not the county sheriff?"

"Where's Abbey?" he asked, still not wanting her to know what had really happened this evening.

"She saw a friend and went to talk to her for a minute. So why Chief Shaffer? From the beginning, that man had it out for you. Remember he's buddy-buddy with the Morgan family."

"Someone shot Kira's front tires."

"Good."

Jessie's anger came through the connection loud and clear. He understood his sister's feelings toward Kira. Her life, as well as his, had been turned upside down because of the trial and his conviction. "Not so good, Jess. The person responsible, I believe, is the killer running around Pinecrest. That's why I'm gonna talk to the chief. He's running the murder investigation."

"How do you know it's the killer? I'm sure prosecutors have a lot of enemies," Jessie said as if she were at the front of the line.

"Not ones who leave messages."

Silence fell.

"Jess, are you there?"

"You really mean he was at our ranch?" Fear weakened her voice.

"Yes. I don't want Abbey to know what happened. Her nightmares are bad enough without adding this latest concern."

"But we aren't safe. On top of everything else, that woman brought the killer to our ranch."

"She doesn't control his actions. No one in Pinecrest is safe with him out there. Stay in the diner, and I'll be there in a while."

When Gabriel disconnected with Jessie, he turned to see the police chief entering the emergency room. Gabriel stiffened, mentally preparing himself for the confrontation sure to take place.

Bill Shaffer stalked to him, a frown slashing across his face. He was only a few years older than Gabriel.

The chief narrowed his eyes, his large bulk barely contained in his blue uniform. "Kira may think you're innocent, but I still think you're as guilty as sin. You made Marcie miserable."

Stay calm. Lord, help here. "Chief Shaffer, you're entitled to your opinion."

"Where's this note that was left in her purse?"

Gabriel gestured to the scrap still on the floor where Kira had dropped it.

Bill took out a handkerchief and picked up the note by one corner. He read the bold black words, his frown strengthening into a scowl. "He's taken a fancy to Kira."

"It looks that way. Now what are you going to do about it?"

The chief's pale gray eyes widened. "Concern for the assistant DA?" Sarcasm dripped from the question. "For all I know you could have put this in her purse as payback."

Gabriel inhaled a composing breath. "That man was at my ranch. I'm concerned for my family and, yes, for any woman in this town."

Bill removed a plastic bag from his pocket and put the note into it. "We'll check for latent prints and any other leads it might give us."

"And?"

"And pray like the dickens we find this man before he strikes again."

"In other words, you don't have many leads." Gabriel ground his teeth together. How had he become the police chief? Marcie's mother handpicked him. That was how. Members of Bill's family worked for Ruth Morgan for years, and his father had been the police chief before him—both pawns for Ruth.

Bill's jaw clamped down as he balled his hands. "There isn't much to go on. Where's Kira?"

"In the exam room. I believe Dr. Addison is in there with her." Gabriel indicated which room with a toss of his head.

The police chief moved to the door of the room and planted himself in the entrance with his arms folded over his barrel chest.

Gabriel needed to leave before the chief decided to take him down to the station for further questioning just to irritate him. He had done what he could for Kira Davis. Now he needed to see to his family.

On the drive to Al's Diner, Gabriel wrestled with his feelings of impotency concerning the investigation of the murders. The killer had involved him on more than one level. He'd been a victim in a lot of ways, but also the man had brought the crime to his doorstep. How could he remain aloof after what happened the past eleven months? He couldn't shake the thought he needed to help Kira. *He* needed to find the murderer.

When he pulled into a parking space in front of the diner, he watched his daughter and sister through the large picture window, talking and laughing at something Al was saying. Because of Abbey and Jessie, he was torn between helping and staying as far away as possible from the investigation. He was just a rancher with a daughter and sister to protect.

He climbed from the cab of his black F-150 and made his way inside the diner that looked like a dive from the outside, but the interior was clean and the food was delicious. Al Nelson had gone to high school with him, a year behind him, and had always loved to cook. No one was surprised when he bought the old café.

Gabriel slipped into the booth next to Abbey and across from Jessie and Al. "How's it going, Al?"

"Not bad. This is the quietest it's been all day."

"Gabriel scanned the diner and noted the five other groups still eating even though it was after nine. Most places shut down early in Pinecrest. "Is the kitchen still open?"

"For you, yes. What's your pleasure?" Al hoisted his tall, thin body from the booth and stood by the table.

Gabriel almost laughed at the word pleasure. He'd had so little of it lately. "Your special is fine by me."

"One beef stew coming up then. Jessie, it was good to see you again. Don't make yourself so scarce. And Abbey, my gal, don't let Bobby think he's getting to you. Smile that pretty smile of yours and walk away. That'll get him."

"Bobby?" Gabriel asked as Al left them alone.

"Oh, he's just a boy at school."

"And?"

"He likes to tease me." Abbey picked up her glass with a chocolate milkshake in it and knocked back the last few sips. She grinned, her mouth ringed with a brown froth. "Don't worry, Daddy. He does it to all the girls."

"So has Al been entertaining y'all?" Gabriel decided to drop the subject of the boy until he got home and could question Jessie alone about Bobby.

"He saw us when he came into the diner and just stopped by the table to say hi." Jessie placed her wadded up paper napkin on her plate, half her meal untouched.

"I thought he was the cook." Gabriel leaned back in the booth.

"Most nights, but he now has someone to help him since the diner's been so popular around here. Ever since his wife left, he's actually taken off more time."

"Good. I know he used to work practically twenty-four/seven."

Jessie began fidgeting with her wadded up napkin, tearing off shreds of paper and littering the table in front of her. "Kinda like someone else I know."

"Daddy, can I get some gum from the vending machine over there?"

"Sure, sweetheart." He dug into his jean pocket and withdrew some coins. When she was gone, he said, "That's part of being a rancher."

"You do have a ranch hand who can help out more."

"I worked hard to buy that land. No one can take care of it as well as me."

Jessie slid a glance at Abbey who started back toward the booth. "No one is more aware of what you sacrificed to have your own ranch. At least Al realized he was heading for a meltdown before it was too late."

Gabriel bit back his reply as Abbey slid in beside him. And all his hard work might be for nothing if he couldn't turn around the losses from this past year.

* * *

Kira lay back on the raised bed, the pain in her head leveling out. The antiseptic smell brought back bad memories. The last time she'd been in the hospital was when her husband had hit her so hard he'd cracked several ribs.

"Kira, what in the world got into you to go to the Michaels' ranch in the dark, alone?" Bill paced the small hospital room, his hands clutching his white cowboy hat so tightly that the material would crinkle when he finally did release his grip.

"It wasn't dark when I arrived." She'd tried to explain to the police chief, but he wouldn't let it go. Bill didn't like Gabriel, still felt he was somehow responsible for Marcie's death, but then Bill cared about what Marcie's mother thought. Bill's mom had been Ruth Morgan's best friend. Whereas Gabriel had been the outsider, the boy from the wrong side of the tracks.

Bill stopped at the window and stared out into the dark. "What did you think you would accomplish?"

"Peace of mind."

He spun about surprisingly fast for such a large man. "You did nothing wrong."

"Tell that to my conscience."

"Kira," he moved to the side of the bed, "what if he's in a partnership with the killer?"

"Not the man I saw today. He isn't that good an actor. Let's face it. The evidence he was convicted on can be explained away if we had looked at other suspects. We homed in on him and didn't look any further. Marcie was found with the other two victims. She died the same way with one bullet through the heart. There were multiple stab wounds before she died and postmortem. They all had the *stop me* note stuffed into their mouths. The same person did all three murders." She paused, her strength fading fast after that fervent outburst. "He's innocent. His conviction was overturned. Move on, Bill," she added in a softer voice.

"I don't like the man. He should never have married Marcie."

"Is that what this is all about?" She dug deep for energy because she needed to make sure the police chief didn't hound Gabriel. The least she could do was make sure he was left alone.

Bill frowned. "Marcie could have done better. You know that."

Kira remembered Marcie's mother yelling at her daughter when she found out she and Gabriel were married. "No, I don't. In spite of his poor beginnings, Gabriel has done well for himself until we threw him in jail. Now, I suspect, all he wants to do is put his life back together."

"What is it about that man that causes the women to go all soft around him? It even happened back in high school when he was getting into trouble."

Kira nearly laughed at that question, but the serious look on the police chief's face stopped her. There was an air of mystery and relentlessness about Gabriel that was intriguing, as though no one had really touched his heart, his soul. In spite of what happened to him, she knew he would rise above and succeed. But then she recalled the vulnerability she glimpsed in his eyes that made a woman want to comfort and hold him, to be that person to get under his skin and truly become a part of him.

"Don't answer. I can see he's gotten to you, too."

"Me?"

"Yes, in the five years as a prosecuting attorney here and in Tulsa, have you ever apologized for doing your job?"

"I've never convicted a person who wasn't guilty."

"That you know about."

Her head throbbed; her body ached. The medication hadn't put a big enough dent in the pain. She massaged her temples. "I'm tired. I'll be at my office tomorrow. Craig just wants to keep me overnight for observation. Let me know anything you find concerning my accident or that note." The words on it flashed into her mind, and she stiffened, her fingernails digging into her palms.

"Fine." Bill strode to the door then turned back. "Don't take unnecessary risks, Kira. You know I don't have the manpower to put someone on you twenty-four hours a day. These cases are eating my lunch as is. I'll make sure a patrol car goes by your house every hour. I'll have the patrol officer check on you at that time. All you have to do is tell him when you're going to bed, and then he'll look around to make sure no one has broken in. Keep your gun close."

As the police chief left, Dr. Craig Addison came into the room. "I wanted to see how you were doing before I went home. How's your head?"

"I know it's there."

"Has the medication helped?"

"It's taken the edge off."

Craig's eyebrows rose. "Really? I can give you something stronger. It'll knock you out and allow you to get a good night's sleep."

There was no way she would take something like that. She'd watched Grams take enough to open her own pharmacy. "I'll be fine. When will you release me?"

"You need to take it easy the next few days. You've got a nasty bump. If you see double, become dizzy or nauseated, let me know immediately."

She'd gone to school with Craig, only two years behind him, and wasn't surprised when he had attended medical school. He'd been the smart boy, always studying. He'd preferred burying his nose in a book to dating. Most people didn't even realize he was in a room because he was so quiet and reserved. "You know me. Much like you, work is my life. Don't worry. I won't do anything I shouldn't."

"I wish I could believe you, but I do

know you." Craig made a clicking sound with his tongue, his hand twisting his stethoscope.

"That's what's bad about coming home. You can't get away with anything."

"This doctor and friend is telling you to rest and take it easy for at least the next forty-eight hours."

When he started to leave, Kira asked, "You'll be here tomorrow morning first thing to release me?"

"I don't know why I even talk to you about what you should do. You won't listen. You're going to the office as soon as you leave, aren't you?"

"No. I need to go home and change first."

Craig shook his head and opened the door. "You're hopeless. A head wound is serious."

For the first time in hours, Kira smiled. Craig and Bill were only concerned for her well-being, but she didn't need a keeper. She needed someone to help her solve these murders. She couldn't help feeling responsible, and she wouldn't rest easy until the right man was locked up.

The swishing sound of the door opening drew her attention. Her heart tripled its rate. Framed in the entrance was Gabriel. His rakishly long black hair was tousled as if he'd run his hand repeatedly through it. His gray eyes held a dangerous glint, and a nerve in his hard jawline twitched. He had the look of a man on a mission.

"Did you see Bill?" she asked, her mouth dry.

"Yes, as I was coming in. He stopped to give me another warning."

"He did?" Bill was as stubborn as Gabriel.

"It seems he fancies himself your protector." Closing the door and shutting the world out, he came into the room.

"He isn't."

"Tell him that."

"I've tried. But he's the police chief and a friend."

"And I'm the guy bent on destroying you."

"Are you?"

"No, even if the chief thinks I am."

Gabriel quickly covered the space between them. Sweat dampened her palms, forehead, and upper lip. Sitting up straight, she clenched her hands at her sides, her mind blank. "I came back to tell you I'll help you with these murders anyway I can. I figure none of us will have our lives back until we've stopped this man. I'll talk to you tomorrow, and we'll start." He stared down at her for an electrifying moment then pivoted and strode to the door.

When he left, all the energy seemed to be siphoned from the room as though a powerful force had swept into her life then swept back out, leaving her wanting more—of what she wasn't sure. Uncurling her hands, she sank back on her pillow, releasing a long sigh. At least she had the help she wanted. For the first time in a long while, hope seeded in her heart.

* * *

"Miss Davis. Miss Davis."

Kira stopped in the hallway near her office at the county courthouse in Pinecrest and glanced at the young man dressed in blue coveralls hurrying toward her. "Hello, Kenny. What can I do for you?"

His freckled face beamed with a smile. "I need to fix your window. When's a good time?"

She checked her watch and realized she didn't have anything urgent this morning. "How about now?"

"I've gotta get my toolbox. I'll be back in a sec."

The custodian scurried down the hall.

After her restless night in the hospital, Kira wished she had his energy. Every sound in the hallway outside her room had played havoc with her imagination. She sighed and continued her trek to her office—three hours later than she usually arrived at work. Grams had picked her up and dropped her off at the courthouse after telling her the whole way that she needed to take better care of herself.

Kira entered her office and greeted her secretary. "Kenny will be coming in to fix that stuck window you've been complaining about."

Penny Carr stopped typing at her computer and looked up. "It's about time. I thought summer would be here before he got around to fixing it."

"You only asked him yesterday morning. Besides, cold weather has never stopped you from opening the window."

"Fresh air is good for the soul."

"And awful for my allergies. Any messages?"

"On your desk except Dickerson Dealership. They just called and said your car was towed there this morning after Chief Shaffer gave the go ahead to move it. It'll be ready for you in a couple of days."

"Good. I'll have transportation soon." With her hand on the doorknob to her inner office, Kira turned back to the older woman who had been the secretary for all the assistant DAs in the county for the past thirty years. "Please don't say anything to Kenny for not getting to the window yesterday. He has his hands full with his mother being so ill."

"Who? Me? I'm the poster woman for good manners," Penny said with a chuckle and began typing again.

Kira shook her head and went into her office. Poster woman for good manners wasn't exactly what she would have said about Penny. Her secretary was a no nonsense woman who didn't tolerate anyone slacking on the job. She knew the functions of the county assistant district attorney's office inside and out. She probably knew the dirty secrets of everyone who worked in this building. Nothing escaped her sharp eye. Kira was lucky to have her as a secretary and would put up with open windows even if the temperature outside was below freezing or above ninety.

Kira plopped her briefcase in her black leather chair and surveyed the stacks of papers on her desk. No little elves had come to do her work in the middle of the night. She picked up one pile and put it on top of the file cabinet behind her to go through later. Then after removing her briefcase, she sat and flipped through her phone messages, massaging her temple where a dull ache persisted in spite of the medication Craig had given her last evening. She was beginning to think it was more stress related.

A knock sounded at her door right before Chief Shaffer stuck his head into her office. "I knew it. I had a bet with Larry that you would be working before noon."

"You should be ashamed of yourself, gambling with one of your men. It's against Oklahoma law."

Bill slipped into the room and closed the door. "I don't want Penny knowing everything."

"If I know Penny, she knew the minute that bet was made."

"Probably even before I decided to make it. Too bad she can't use that special ability of hers to find out who the murderer is."

Suddenly the light mood evaporated, and Kira put her messages down. "What did you find out about my car?"

"In addition to four holes in your car frame, there are two bullets in one tire and a third in another. I have an officer combing the area at the Michaels' ranch for any more."

"Do they match the ones found in the women?"

"Yes. The striae on the bullets came from the same weapon used in the murders."

She'd known it in her gut, but to have it confirmed left her shaken to the core. She folded her hands in her lap and tried to appear calm. "Did you find anything useful from the note?"

"Not from it or from your purse, which I'm returning to you." He placed her leather bag on top of the tallest stack of papers. "I think you'll be safe here at the courthouse. Call me when you want to go home. I'll have Larry escort you to and from the courthouse."

"The murderer didn't contact his victims before he killed them."

"We don't know that for sure."

"I mean something else to him. If he'd wanted me dead, I would be. He had the perfect opportunity last night." Cold swept through her as if she'd opened her office window.

"Maybe. But this scum—guy doesn't think like you or me. No telling what he's up to."

With those words, the police chief left her office. Kira lifted her trembling hands from her lap and tried to work, but mental images of the women's mutilated bodies kept stealing her concentration. Covering her face with her palms, she leaned her elbows on the desktop, acknowledging that she could be the killer's next victim in spite of what she'd said to Bill. But she could say that about any young woman in town. They all needed protecting.

"He's here."

Kira jerked upright and looked at Penny inside her door. She hadn't even heard it open. "Who?"

"Gabriel Michaels. You had some trouble at his ranch last night. Do you think he's here about that?"

"You mean you don't know? This has got to be a first."

"I thought it could be about the fight he had with Marcie's brother this morning. He probably wants to press charges. Josh

Morgan just came at Gabriel for no reason."

"Gabriel was in a fight this morning?"

"It's Gabriel, is it?"

"We went to school together."

"Isn't he three years older than you?"

"Yes, but—" Kira caught the mischievous gleam in Penny's eyes and clamped her mouth shut, determined not to reveal another thing to the woman.

"I'll show him in."

Kira took a swift glance around her office and wished she wasn't such a messy person. She knew where everything was, but it would be hard for anyone to believe that when he looked at the disarray scattered everywhere. She ran a hand through her blond hair, felt the tender lump over her eye, and wondered if her lipstick was still on.

As Gabriel entered, his gaze riveted to hers for a few, long seconds before he scanned her office, one brow lifting. "I pictured you neat and organized with a place for everything."

"I know where everything is. There's organization in this chaos."

He closed the door and eased into the chair in front of her desk. She'd always felt her office was an adequate size until this moment. Suddenly the room shrank, and she was very aware of being alone with him.

"The police were at my ranch at the crack of dawn. What did they find out about the car?"

"The gun used was the same caliber as the one used to kill the women, but there wasn't anything on the note."

"I would have been surprised if there had been." He leaned forward. "What can I do to help?"

"I need to know everything you can think of concerning Marcie. She was our first victim."

"That you know of."

"You think there are other bodies out there at a different burial site?"

He shrugged. "It's possible. You might look into women from this county or the surrounding ones who've been reported missing in the past few years."

"I'll see if Bill has. I don't know what

I'm looking for, but the man killing these women is from around here. He isn't some transient passing through. Maybe somehow Marcie sparked this killing spree. Did she have any enemies?"

"Besides me?"

"Were you two enemies?"

He glanced out the window for a long moment. "Our divorce negotiations weren't without animosity, but believe it or not, I didn't hate Marcie at all. I felt sorry for her."

"Why?"

"Nothing made her happy for long."

"Her family tried to come up with a list, and all they could think of was you. They felt everyone loved Marcie. Apparently not. Can you think of others?"

"You were her best friend all the way through school. When you came back to town, y'all picked right back up. Did she have any enemies?"

"There was Shirley in high school. She hated Marcie for always getting the guys. Besides her, I don't know of anyone else, but then I was gone for nine years. So, do you think these murders are random or connected?"

His gaze slid away from hers then back. "I've been thinking about last year. Marcie was seeing someone while we were legally separated, maybe before that."

FOUR

Kira straightened. "Who did Marcie have the affair with? You never mentioned she was seeing someone else while you two were still married."

"I tried, but the police wouldn't listen, so I kept my mouth shut. Having an unfaithful wife can be considered a good motive for murder. I didn't want to strengthen your case anymore than it was."

"I want to know now and would have if I'd known you'd said that. Who?" This could be a lead, especially since it wasn't common knowledge Marcie was having an affair.

He shook his head, his eyebrows

slashing downward. "She wouldn't say. But she did enjoy taunting me about the fact."

"You never followed her or anything to discover the man's identity?"

"By that time, I didn't care. But if I'd known I needed someone else as a prospective killer, I would have." His look narrowed on her. "Marcie wasn't good about keeping secrets. Are you sure she didn't say anything about being interested in another man?"

"No, and I thought we shared everything."

"Obviously not."

Marcie had kept her own secrets as Kira had from her. The realization she hadn't known about Marcie's secret liaison shook her faith even more in being able to read people. She'd always felt she could, but this whole situation from Gabriel's arrest to now made her acknowledge she could be wrong about a lot of things. She certainly had been about her ex-husband. She was discovering everything wasn't black and white.

"Marcie had a way of excluding people

who cared about her from her life."

Kira tapped her pen against the blotter. "If you could make an educated guess, who do you think it was?"

"A man who had something to hide. Otherwise I think she would have flaunted her affair. She didn't care what others thought."

"A married man?"

"Maybe. Didn't her journal ever talk about the man?"

"No. There were some entries that referred to a *he*, but that was all. I was surprised when the police found her journals. I thought she'd stopped after high school." Had Gabriel read any of Marcie's entries?

"She used to stay up late putting her thoughts down on paper."

"And you were never tempted to read it?"

His mouth firmed in a harsh line. "No. I always respected her privacy."

"I'm sorry. I didn't mean to accuse you of anything." Kira shifted several folders from one pile to another. "We need to find out who Marcie was seeing?'

"You're thinking he could be the killer?"

"Maybe. Or he might know something but not want to come forward."

"I would like to read her journals. There might be something in them that will give us a lead."

Kira remembered the passages that referred to Gabriel and frowned. "I don't know if that's a good idea."

"Give me a break. You don't think she let me know exactly what she thought of me those last months we were together? I doubt anything she wrote would be worse than what she said to my face."

Kira chewed on her bottom lip, her pen tapping at a faster pace. She recalled some of the passages and again realized she hadn't really known the woman who wrote them. The depths of Marcie's hatred had poured off those pages. "If you're sure."

"Yes. I want this person caught."

"I'll have to get them from the police chief. We can meet at my place tonight."

He nodded. "Are you going to tell him why?"

"No. He doesn't need to know you'll be reading them, too. I already know how he feels about you. I want to reread the journals in light of the knowledge that Marcie was seeing someone without anyone knowing—which is hard to accomplish in a small town."

"Won't the chief think it's strange you want them? Usually the prosecutors don't get involved in a case until it goes to trial."

"Whether I like it or not, I am involved. The killer has chosen to involve me. Your false conviction has made me a participant in this investigation. I won't let the wrong man be accused again."

"Such passion. That was part of the reason I was sent to prison. I can still remember your closing remarks at my trial. If any juror had doubt, he didn't after you sat down."

His words hit her like a slap. Beneath the surface, his anger still simmered, ready at a moment's notice to boil over and scald her. She should be afraid of him, but for some reason, she wasn't, in spite of her bad judgment of some people in the past.

She remembered him comforting her the night before. There was compassion and gentleness in this man Marcie had claimed was a brute who only wanted his own way.

"I wouldn't have been appointed by the district DA if I didn't put one hundred percent of myself into the job."

His intense scrutiny captured her full attention. "Do you do everything in life with that kind of approach?"

Her throat dry, she swallowed hard. "Yes."

For a long moment he said nothing. Kira wiped her damp palms on her skirt. Different emotions flitted across his face. He was wrestling with himself, coming to a decision that, for some reason, she sensed would shift their relationship.

"Have you had lunch yet?"

"No. And I skipped the wonderful breakfast they served at the hospital." The tightness in her stomach had nothing to do with hunger and everything to do with the man sitting across from her.

"Al's Diner isn't far. Want to grab something to eat and continue our discussion about Marcie's lover?"

She needed to eat, and she wanted people to see Gabriel with the assistant DA. There were still some in town who thought him guilty because that was what the Morgan family wanted. She, at least, owed him her support. She wouldn't be used by the Morgans ever again. "That'll be fine. I can't be long. I have a meeting at one."

Gabriel pushed to his feet. "I have an appointment, too, before I pick up Abbey at school."

"She doesn't ride the bus?"

"Usually she does, but I knew I would be in town today, so I told her to wait at school for me."

"I enjoyed seeing her again last night. I wish it had been under better circumstances. Every time I see her, I think about Marcie when we were growing up."

"She's nothing like her mother," Gabriel clipped out each word, his jaw set, his tension conveyed in his stance.

"She looks exactly like her mother."

"And that's where the resemblance ends." A storm brewed in the depths of his eyes.

"No matter what you feel about Marcie, she's still Abbey's mother." Kira came from behind her desk, all too aware that the friend she was defending hadn't been the best example for her daughter.

Gabriel blocked Kira's path to the door, tall and indomitable, a man protecting what was his. "Don't tell me how to raise my daughter. The Morgans have already tried that."

"I wouldn't dream of it." She stood her ground, her own tension making her rigid. "But I do know that Marcie loved Abbey."

"Marcie only loved herself. That last month before she disappeared, she didn't see Abbey half the time she was supposed to. That devastated my daughter."

She started to protest, but some of what she'd read in Marcie's journals supported Gabriel's accusation. She'd moved into town to live, and although she was nearer to Kira, Marcie kept backing out of plans. Apparently she'd done the same with her daughter. Because of the man she was seeing?

"She used my daughter to get back at me. I won't let Abbey be used like that again."

Bitterness laced his voice, but also the pain. What had happened to Marcie? How could she have been so blind to what Marcie had been doing? Kira touched his arm. "I'm sorry."

He looked down at her fingers. When his gaze returned to her face, he'd cloaked his expression. She started to remove her hand, but he clasped it, the rough texture of his skin a vivid reminder of the very essence of the man.

She ran her tongue over her dry lips. "What happened? What went wrong?"

"I wouldn't do what she wanted, so she was going to make sure I paid. Her family had wanted me to come into their business. I refused and bought the ranch instead. She hated it and let me know how she felt all the time. I suppose the day I bought the ranch was the day my marriage really ended even though we remained married for four more years. I wanted it to work because of our daughter. Marcie didn't care. She wanted a big house, things I couldn't give her."

"She knew who you were when you two married. She was only rebelling against her family. She thought it would be fun to marry beneath her. Her words not mine."

He twisted away from Kira and moved toward the door. "My father had worked for hers. She took pleasure in telling me that on a number of occasions."

"Wait."

He threw her a glance over his shoulders. "I'm hungry and this conversation is over." He thrust open the door, stepped into the outer office, and tipped his cowboy hat at Penny.

Kira grabbed her purse and followed, disturbed by the picture Gabriel painted of her old friend. When she had returned to Pinecrest to fill in the vacancy of the county assistant DA, she hadn't seen Marcie much in the years since high school. She looked the same—beautiful, prideful, but there had been a hard edge to her that Kira had thought had been put there by Gabriel and a failing marriage. Now she wasn't so sure.

When Kira emerged from her office, Kenny was working by the large window with his toolbox. He grinned at her and stopped.

"I'll have this window fixed in no time, Miss Davis."

"I appreciate that. My secretary loves fresh air. Penny, I'll be at Al's Diner."

"You have a one o'clock with the mayor."

"Yes, I know." Just the mention of the mayor caused the dull ache behind her eyes to throb even more. Every day he demanded a solution to three murders, a solution that neither she nor the police had.

As Kira walked beside Gabriel across the street to the diner, several people stopped to stare. When they entered the place, a few customers turned to look while they strode to the booth in front of the picture window.

"There's a table in the back if you want to be less conspicuous." Gabriel remained standing.

She glanced at him and smiled. "No, this is perfect. I have a statement to make for the doubters of this town."

Gabriel slid into the booth across from her. "I don't need you to fight my battles."

"I know. I'm doing this for myself."

"It doesn't change the past."

"I know that, too." Her stomach knotted. Nothing could undo what happened.

Tension had grown between them, starting when they crossed the street. With each look they had received, Gabriel had drawn more into himself, his expression more solemn the closer they got to the restaurant until his stress was a palpable force erecting a barrier between them.

After she scanned the menu, Kira placed her order with the waitress, wondering if she would be able to eat any of the meal. She needed to get the conversation away from what happened to Gabriel. That would always be between them, but if they were going to work together, she wanted a truce.

"Can you forget the past year for the time we need to work together?" Being direct was her usual way of dealing with any unpleasant situations. She hated playing games.

His sharp gaze bored through her. "As though it never happened?"

"I know it's something you'll never really forget, but can you put it aside for the time being? It's hard to concentrate with all this tension between us."

A nerve jerked in his jaw. "Can you forget about something as life changing just like"—he snapped his finger—"that?"

Flashes of memories of Jonathan's verbal and in the end physical abuse captured her mind. For a moment, she was transported back in time to their final confrontation that led to her divorce. The sound of the slap against her cheek that sent her tumbling down the stairs echoed through her thoughts. She couldn't forget or forgive it even though Grams kept telling her that was the only way she could really move forward.

She looked right at him. "No."

Silence hung between them until the waitress set their coffee mugs on the table.

"I'm not sure this can work if—"

"I'll try, Kira. That's all I can promise."

"Thanks." Relieved, she lounged back.

Al put the hamburgers down in front of them. "When I heard you were out here, I wanted to say hi, Kira, and to see how you're doing. I heard about your run-in with the killer yesterday."

She forced a smile. What else were people saying? "News travels fast."

Al towered over them, glaring at Gabriel. "Well, not from this guy. I can't believe you were in here last night and didn't tell me what happened at your ranch. I had to hear it from Penny today at breakfast."

"Abbey was with me." Gabriel dumped a packet of sugar into his coffee.

"Oh, yeah. I guess that wouldn't be a good topic with your daughter around. Are you okay, Kira? I heard you were in the hospital overnight."

"I'm better."

"Good. I need to get back to the kitchen." Al gave her a smile then left. The owner of the café was all arms and legs, and when he moved, it was with an

103

awkward gait as though he couldn't get his limbs to work together.

"I'm surprised he came out to say anything." Kira squirted mustard on her bun. "He doesn't talk much even here in the diner. I remember him being painfully shy in school. Wasn't he the one who threw up in English class when the teacher made him get up in front of the class to read his report?"

"Yes. That flew around the school faster than lightning. He's still shy, but because he owns this place, he's really trying to overcome that. I heard he took speech at night school, but it was a disaster."

"It was sweet of him to ask about last night."

"Odd, though. His behavior last night was odd, too. When I came to pick up Abbey and Jessie, he was sitting at the table talking to them, even laughing. That's not like him. I didn't think too much about it at the time. I had more important things on my mind."

"Like what?"

"Whether I was going to help you or

not."

"I'm glad you did. For the first time I have hope something will break for us. This clue about a lover has potential."

"If we can figure out who it is." Gabriel lavished ketchup on his French fries.

"I'll get the journals later today. After we read them, we might have a better feel for who the guy is. I haven't looked at them since your trial."

"Knowing Marcie and what she told me she wanted, he had to be rich, successful, and willing to indulge her every whim."

Pain filled his words, and she wasn't even sure that Gabriel was aware of it. He tried to act as if Marcie's affair hadn't bothered him, but it had. She saw it in his eyes. Was he still in love with her? Love and hate were such strong emotions, easily mixed up. Jonathan had said he loved her repeatedly, but his actions showed her the opposite.

"How's the ranch doing?" Kira took a bite of her hamburger, relishing the juicy meat with Al's special sauce cooked in.

"Hank and Jessie did what they could to

keep it going while I was in prison. She tried to hire some extra help, but no one would work for them or if they did, they didn't stay more than a couple of days."

"Why didn't you sell the ranch?"

Gabriel tunneled his fingers through his dark hair. "I wasn't ready to acknowledge defeat. I was innocent. I kept hoping someone would figure it out. And finally the Lord answered my prayers."

She used to go regularly to church, but once Jonathan's verbal abuse intensified, she only went to work. Anywhere else required she pretend everything was all right when it wasn't. During those years, she'd prayed to God to help her. Her situation only worsened until she decided she was on her own.

"Your sister is quite devoted to you. After the trial and again yesterday, she let me know in no uncertain terms exactly how she felt about your conviction."

"Yeah, she can be a fierce tigress. She was the one who kept Hank going. I think he would have given up last spring when we had that unexpected heavy snowfall that took weeks to melt."

"Are you going to try to hire more help now that you've been vindicated?"

"Right now, he's the only one I can afford. But that's gonna change. My ranch is my daughter's legacy. I intend to make it a success despite what the Morgan family wants."

The strain, which had eased, sprang up between them again. Kira finished chewing her last bite of her hamburger. "I heard you had a run in with Josh this morning."

"News does travel fast in this town. Penny?"

"Yeah, who else? What did you two fight about?"

"Abbey." Gabriel ate several fries, his gaze trained on a spot in front of the diner. "He doesn't think I have the best interests of my daughter at heart."

"Why? It's obvious to anyone who sees you two together that you do." She could easily envy Abbey. The girl knew her father and that he loved her. Kira couldn't say the same thing about her own dad and that hurt.

He didn't look at her but said, "He doesn't think Abbey's safe at the ranch. He thinks that his family is better equipped to protect her and keep her safe, especially with what happened yesterday."

"Is she safe?" The question slipped out while she thought about what she'd gone through so close to his home.

He stiffened, his jaw set in a firm line that spoke of a man grappling with a problem. "Is anyone safe in Pinecrest? I don't know. But I do know that I'll protect her with my life. I can't say that about Josh. Marcie's family cares for themselves before anyone else. I learned that painful lesson the hard way."

"So what did you tell him?"

He winced. "I don't care to repeat it, but I'm sure he got my point."

"Is that when he punched you?"

"That's when he tried to."

Kira chuckled. "I'd have liked to have seen that."

"You mean you aren't one of the hordes of women lining up to go out with him?"

"I know too much about the man."

"That sounds intriguing. Too bad I have a meeting at the bank in twenty minutes."

* * *

Along with dozens of other parents waiting in their cars, Gabriel sat impatiently staring at the school's front doors, willing his daughter to come out. From the crowd, he realized he wasn't the only one afraid for his child to come home alone.

While the first group of children raced from the building, he thumped his forefinger against the steering wheel. A mental vision of Kira formed as the minutes slowly ticked down. Surprisingly, when he thought about her, none of his earlier anger materialized. Maybe he would be able to move past this last year, at least where Kira was concerned. She was a beautiful woman who...

What was he thinking? He could never be interested in Kira Davis. He could never trust her, especially after Marcie.

Gabriel forced any thought of Kira from his mind and concentrated on finding

Abbey in the horde of children leaving the building. Finally, when the trickle of kids stopped coming out of the front doors, he gripped the steering wheel, fighting the wave of alarm rushing through him.

Where are you?

He thrust open his door and hurried toward the entrance. His heart pounded as quickly as his booted feet against the concrete. The buses were leaving, the parents in their cars almost all gone, and his daughter was nowhere to be found. At the front door, he paused and panned the lawn, praying he was panicking for no reason, that he would find his daughter by his truck, waving and smiling at him. But all he saw was one boy pedaling away from the school.

Gabriel pivoted around and yanked open the doors. His pace down the long empty corridor quickened as he neared his destination. *Please let Abbey be in in the principal's office, safe.*

When he entered the main office, he found only one older woman behind the counter. He approached her. "Where's

Abbey Michaels?"

The woman screwed her face into a thoughtful expression and tilted her head to the side. "She isn't here."

"What do you mean Abbey isn't here?" Gabriel tried to remain calm by inhaling a deep, composing breath to still the rapid thumping of his heartbeat, but he felt his control slipping.

Principal Evan Jones came out of his office and crossed to the counter. "Mr. Michaels, Mrs. Morgan picked up her granddaughter about thirty minutes ago."

Relieved, Gabriel relaxed the tense set of his body for a brief second until he realized who had his daughter. "I didn't give my permission for Mrs. Morgan to take Abbey today."

The principal shifted from one foot to the other, his features pulled into a worried expression. "I just assumed since she was Abbey's grandmother that it was okay. She's picked her up in the past."

Gabriel glared at the muscular man who looked as though he had stepped off the cover of Gentleman's Quarterly. "Well, you assumed wrong, Mr. Jones. Jessie Michaels or I are the only ones allowed to pick up Abbey. Is that understood?"

"Yes, you've made yourself perfectly clear."

Gabriel wanted to punch the man in the mouth to wipe that sudden smug look from his face, to mess that perfect hair that probably was never out of place even in a windstorm. Instead, Gabriel swung away from the counter and walked from the office, his long strides eating up the distance to his truck. He jerked the door open and climbed inside.

He slammed his palm against the steering wheel. Pain raced up his arm. The less he saw his ex-mother-in-law the better off he was. She wanted Abbey and would stop at nothing to get her—even kidnapping—and somehow she would get away with it.

After throwing the truck into reverse, he backed out of the parking space and headed for the Morgan's estate on the outskirts of town. If it were possible, he would storm into the house, grab Abbey, and escape before he had to say a word to Ruth Morgan. He was afraid of what would come out of his mouth. Rage built each mile closer to the white mansion as he recalled each angry comment, each threat she had issued, especially since Marcie's disappearance last January.

At the front door, he paused to calm himself, to tell himself all the reasons he must not let Marcie's family get to him. Then he rang the bell and waited. His heartbeat quickened its pace with each second that passed.

A maid opened the door, her eyes growing wide, but she didn't stop him from entering. Nor did she stand in his way when he heard voices and headed toward the sounds. He came to a halt inside the den. Abbey poured tea for her grandmother as though she went to a girl's finishing school and Amy Vanderbilt had personally instructed her in what was proper.

"Sugar?" Abbey held up the bowl.

Ruth shook her head.

Abbey spooned some sugar into her cup and stirred, her gaze finally fastening on

Gabriel. "Daddy." She forgot everything her grandmother had taught her and raced unladylike to him, throwing her arms around his waist and hugging him.

Gabriel tousled her hair. "Are you ready to leave?" He swung his attention to Ruth while he spoke to his daughter.

The woman with brown hair in a bun pulled herself up to a ramrod stance and managed to look down upon him even though he towered over her by a good foot. "Abigail, please find Sara and tell her to give you some of those special cookies you like so much."

Abbey glanced from him to her grandmother, indecision on her face as her teeth dug into her bottom lip. "Daddy?"

"Go find Sara. I'll be along in a minute to get you. Ruth and I have a few things to talk about." He smiled at Abbey as if he had not a care in the world while inside he raged at the woman not ten feet from him.

When Abbey was gone, Ruth indicated with a wave of her hand for him to be seated across from her. He remained where he was, forcing her to stand, too. She squared her thin shoulders even more, her back stiffening until he thought she would snap in two pieces. That haughty look she reserved for him descended.

"You are not to take Abbey without my permission. I am still her father."

"I have a right to see my granddaughter."

"As much as I would like to deny you that, I won't. Abbey loves you, and I won't hurt her by using her to get back at you, but you'll play by *my* rules."

Her piercing ice blue eyes became pinpoints. "Only until we go to court."

"You think a judge is going to erase the fact that I'm Abbey's father?"

The woman's eyes frosted. "If there's justice in this world, yes. I can give her everything. You can't." She glanced away a few seconds then brought her glacial gaze back to his face. "But today, I brought Abbey home because I knew you would come for her. We need to talk about my granddaughter."

"No, we don't." He began to leave before he did something he would regret.

"Abbey is in danger."

Those words stopped him, and he swung back toward the woman.

"I heard what happened at your ranch yesterday. Abbey has been exposed to the killer. She shouldn't be at the ranch where he could get to her."

"Over my dead body." If the gun used yesterday hadn't been the murder weapon, he would think that Ruth Morgan had hired someone to scare Kira and him. She was capable of that, but he didn't think she was capable of having three women murdered, especially her own daughter.

"As much as I would like that, I wouldn't want Abigail to end—" She swallowed, some of the stiffness siphoning from her body. "I never want Abigail to suffer like Marcie did. It's possible the killer could murder you then her. He might take a fancy to her because she looks so much like...Marcie."

The force of her logic struck him. If the killer did that, he would never... "I can protect her."

"Can you?" One delicate eyebrow

arched.

"You think you can do better than me?" The scorn he couldn't keep hidden any longer dripped from his question. He let his look trail down the length of her petite, frail frame. He took a step closer.

"Yes."

"How?"

"I'll take her away from here until the killer is caught. I know of a place in Florida on the beach with topnotch security. She'll love it. It will be an adventure for her, and she'll be safe because no one else will know about this place. I'd hire a tutor for her until she can return to school here."

His need for Abbey in his life urged him to shout, "No. It's Christmas in a few weeks."

"For once, put aside your pride and selfish needs to see what's best for Abbey. Do you want her to end up like..." Ruth cleared her throat, a glistening sheen in her blue eyes that took the bite out of their coldness, "...like Marcie?"

What if his ex-mother-in-law took Abbey away, and he never saw her again?

What if the killer came after his daughter, and he couldn't protect her? His life would be over. It was that simple. Nothing, no one could harm his daughter. She was all he really had. He would do anything to see that didn't happen—even let her grandmother take her to a safe haven. The pain deep inside pushed outward until the constriction in his chest threatened to double him over. His lungs on fire, he couldn't breathe decently.

"What will it be?"

Ruth's voice penetrated his thought as he struggled with what he knew he had to do. "She can go with you on one condition."

Again one of her eyebrows quirked as if she couldn't believe he dared to lay down conditions to her.

"My sister must accompany you."

"I don't need another—"

"If you want Abbey to go, then Jessie has to go, too. There's no other way I'll let her be with you. I know Jessie will see that my daughter is returned to me."

"Are you implying I would kidnap my own granddaughter?"

"Yes, if you thought you could get away with it, I think you would just to spite me for marrying Marcie."

She pulled herself up straight again, that haughty look on her face. "Very well, I accept your condition. I want to leave this evening."

So soon? He wasn't ready to say good-bye to Abbey. He'd just been released from prison a week ago. Gabriel opened his mouth to protest but didn't. He had to let her go and immediately, especially after the night before at his ranch. But it hurt as if he'd been shot in the gut and left to bleed out.

"I'll be back with her clothes."

FIVE

Gabriel stood in the middle of Abbey's bedroom at the ranch, staring at the suitcase open on her bed. He didn't want to let her go. A war between his mind and heart stormed inside of him.

God, what are You doing? I just came back into Abbey's life. I...

Nothing else came into his thoughts. He couldn't even express his feelings to the Lord. He curled his hands then uncurled them over and over. Frozen, unable to think or move, he closed his eyes. Her grandmother had bought most of Abbey's clothes in the bag when his daughter lived with her. Even her favorite toys were new ones from Ruth. When he came home, all he'd been able to do was shower love on her since he'd returned. What little money he had went to food and keeping the ranch running. And now he wouldn't even be able to do that.

The sound of a door slamming penetrated his pity party. He didn't have a choice. Abbey and Jessie's well-being was more important than what he felt or wanted.

Footsteps stomped in the direction of Abbey's bedroom and came to a stop. He pivoted toward Jessie, framed in the doorway.

Her glare burned through him. "I don't want to go with that woman. We'll be okay. I know how to shoot, and I'll protect Abbey with my life."

"That's what I'm afraid of. I know how you feel about Ruth Morgan, but I can't send Abbey without you. I don't trust the woman. I need you and Abbey to be safe. I'm going after this maniac. This past hellish year began because of him."

The color drained from his sister's face.

"No. I can't lose you, too. The Morgan family is responsible for Mama's death. All they thought about after Marcie's death was making you pay for being married to her."

"Mama had a heart attack."

"From the stress. You and I both know that. She wouldn't take care of herself. She was so despondent, and her sugar and blood pressure levels were off the charts."

His mother had never been a strong woman. Gabriel could place as much blame on himself as he could the Morgan family. If he hadn't married Marcie...He shook his head, stalked to the bed, and closed the suitcase. "We need to go. Where's your bag?"

Jessie pressed her mouth into a thin line.

"You did pack, didn't you?" He was so tired of fighting. That was all he'd done this past year—actually since a couple of years after his marriage to Marcie. He wanted peace and to be left alone.

"It's by the front door."

"I'll call you every day." He hefted the

suitcase and strode into the hallway. "I know this won't be easy for you, but Abbey does love her grandmother. And in Ruth's own way, she loves Abbey."

"What about you? We can't lose you. Let the police do their job."

Gabriel opened the front door, took Jessie's piece of luggage, and waited while his sister walked outside. "How has that worked so far? We have three dead women, and they locked me up for a crime I didn't do. They had their chance." He swung the suitcases up into the bed of his truck.

"And you think Chief Shaffer will stand by while you investigate?"

"I'll let Kira deal with him."

As Gabriel started the engine, Jessie said, "How can you work with her after what she did to you?"

He'd already asked himself that question while wrestling with his decision to help her or not. "It's hard to explain. I feel like I have to. We both know Marcie better than anyone else. She was the first victim. That may be important. What caused the killer to start with her?"

"Aren't you angry with Kira? Hate her?"

"Yes and no. I don't have the mental energy to hate her right now. All I want to do is keep my family safe, and if that means figuring out with her who's murdering these women, then I'll do it. I'm not leaving my life in anyone else's hands ever again."

For the next ten minutes, his sister remained quiet. At a stop sign near the estate, Gabriel glanced at her.

Silent tears ran down her face.

"Jessie, you're strong. You'll hold your own with Ruth."

His sister swiped her hands across her cheeks. "I'm not worried about me. I'm worried about you."

At the entrance to the Morgan estate, he punched the button to call the main house. While the gates opened, he clasped Jessie's shoulder. "I'll be fine. I have the best reason to stay alive. I don't want Ruth to raise Abbey, especially after how Marcie turned out. Her mother dictated Marcie's actions most of her life and look what happened."

"Sure. I'll turn off my emotions." Jessie shrugged away from his touch. "Let's get this over with. I want to be home before Christmas."

"That's my goal, too." The holidays without his family would be bleak—like this past year.

Gabriel parked in front of the mansion and trudged to the entrance with the two pieces of luggage.

Josh, Marcie's brother, opened the door and stepped to the side. His gaze bore through Gabriel and lit on Jessie. Josh's scowl deepened the grooves on his forehead. Gabriel and Jessie entered the large entry hall with a massive staircase.

In all the years married to Marcie, he'd rarely been to the second floor, but then he'd never been welcomed in the house. "Where's Abbey?"

"In the living room with Mother. Now that you're finally arrived, I'll let our pilot know we're leaving."

"So you're going, too?" Gabriel asked, staring at the man's black eye Gabriel had given him. That was a testament to their relationship from the very beginning.

Marcie's brother gave one nod.

While Josh left, Jessie leaned close to Gabriel. "Oh, joy. He's going with us."

"Shh. Remember Abbey adores her uncle."

"Did you when you hit Josh?"

Gabriel chuckled. "I tried, but I couldn't stop myself. I have to defend myself."

Jessie harrumphed and followed her brother to the living room.

The second Abbey saw him she leaped to her feet and raced across the enormous room, more like a museum than a home. She threw her arms around Gabriel's waist. "You've got to come, too. I don't wanna go alone without you."

He set the suitcases on the floor then knelt in front of his daughter, forcing a smile to his face while inside he felt anything but happy. "Sweetheart, I wish I could. Someone has to take care of the ranch. That's why Jessie is going with you. We'll talk every day."

"Promise?"

"Yes. I'll want to hear all about what you're doing."

"How long will I be away? It's gonna be Christmas soon. We're always together then." Abbey dropped her head and stared at her hands folded together in front of her.

"And we will be this year." Somehow he'd find the killer by then. He couldn't let Abbey down anymore. "You'll have a great time at the beach. Look for some shells while there. You could start a collection."

His daughter's shoulder slumped forward. "Please come. I don't want to leave you." She wrapped her arms around his neck and clung to him.

A heavy sadness jammed his throat, and no amount of swallowing pushed it down. A blurry film covered his eyes as he embraced Abbey as though this was the last time he would see her. He wanted to be the one taking his daughter and sister away, but catching the killer was paramount, and he couldn't depend on anyone but himself to do it.

Josh came into the room. "Time to go."

Gabriel loosened his embrace and

began to stand, but Abbey wouldn't let go.

"No! I don't wanna go." Tears streaked down his daughter's face.

"Honey, I need you to," he whispered into her ear while giving her one final hug.

Ruth stood behind Abbey.

Gabriel's gaze met the frost in the woman's eyes. The sight almost changed his mind.

But then Ruth bent toward his daughter, clasping her shoulder. "You should see what I have planned for you and your aunt. The time will fly by."

Abbey turned her head toward her grandmother, whose smile encompassed her whole face. Gabriel used the momentary distraction to pull away from Abbey and nod toward his sister.

Jessie stepped forward. "I've never been to the beach. You'll have to show me everything, Abbey."

While her grandmother and aunt flanked his daughter, Gabriel backed away. "Have fun, sweetheart. I love you." Then he spun around and hurried across the foyer and out of the mansion.

Abbey's cries for him to return ripped his heart in two. But if he went back, he wouldn't let her go, and then she would be in danger. He was doing the right thing, but if he had to tear this town apart, he would find the killer.

* * *

Kira faced the stack of Marcie's journals and set the one written as a high school senior in a read pile off to the side. She thought it might help if she went through them in chronological order this time rather than how she'd done it when planning her prosecution of Gabriel.

Marcie's had written in a journal since she'd been a freshman. Kira had also but not to the extent her friend had, and Kira gave it up after high school. A lot of what Marcie put down had to do with her family, especially about her mother, until her junior year. Then she became enthralled with any guy her mother didn't like. When she could finally date at eighteen, she made it a point never to go out with boys acceptable to her mother.

Eleven months ago, Kira had combed through them, seeing a side of her best friend Kira hadn't really known until she returned to town. At first, she'd thought the change had come about because of her marriage to Gabriel, but now she didn't really know. She'd gone through the one dated during her last months in high school, and what she'd finished had a different tone. Now that Kira wasn't looking for ways to convict Gabriel, the meaning behind the passages weren't the same as she'd thought last winter.

A month before graduation, Marcie set her eyes on Gabriel and went after him as though she was a predator homing in on her prey. Subtle changes in her language shifted. She'd been attracted to him because she'd known her mother would never approve. Kira saw traces of evidence that Marcie cared for Gabriel—at least at first. By the summer after graduation, Marcie was really falling in love with him.

She reached for the next journal written after Kira left for college. The ringing doorbell startled her, and she flinched. She glanced at her watch. Gabriel was late. In fact she'd wondered an hour ago if he'd decided not to help her.

Clutching the chronicle to her chest, she headed for the entry hall. It was ten o'clock. She leaned toward the peephole, surprised that it was Gabriel. She'd half expected a police officer checking in with her.

Hurriedly opening the door, she noticed a patrolman striding toward the house. Gabriel locked gazes with her for a few seconds then glanced over his shoulder. The officer increased his pace, and Kira recognized Wally, one of Bill's cronies.

She came out onto the porch, putting herself between Gabriel and Wally. "Thanks for stopping by. I'm fine."

Wally paused at the bottom of the stairs, his hand resting on his gun at his waist. "Are you sure?" He pinned his stare on Gabriel behind her.

"I'm *very* sure. He will be here for a while so you don't need to come up to the door if you see his truck in the driveway."

"I have my orders, ma'am. The chief won't be too happy if I don't follow them."

"And I don't need a babysitter as long as Gabriel is here."

Officer Wally Byrd tipped his cowboy hat, threw one last glare toward Gabriel, and strode to his patrol car. Gabriel was not the killer, and he didn't need to be treated as if he was. Kira took a step forward, intending to have a private word with the man.

Gabriel clasped her arm. "Don't on my account. Nothing you say will change some people's mind."

She whirled around. "It should. If the police don't put one hundred percent behind catching the murderer, he'll go scot free."

His strong jawline twitched. "That's why I'm not depending on the police. I'm going to find the killer. Let's get started." Without waiting for her, he entered her house.

Heart still thumping against her rib cage, she followed. She hated injustice. She stomped through the entrance and slammed the door, hoping the officer heard. She walked into the living room and checked out the front window. The patrol car was still there.

She jerked the drapes closed and decided she couldn't let the man get to her. When she turned to Gabriel, he stood in front of the stack of journals. "I've started going through the ones in high school. I'd like you to read the newest to the oldest ones. If anything jumps out at you, put it down on a piece of paper. Then we can compare notes. We can do part tonight and the rest tomorrow night if that works for you."

"No, it doesn't." He slanted a look at her. "We need to go through them in one sitting. Time is against us."

"Then why didn't you come earlier?"

"I had business to tend to."

"But this is important."

"So is my family."

"I know you haven't been around Abbey and Jessie much these past months. I could have come to the ranch." As she said the last sentence, she shuddered, remembering the last time and wanting to snatch the

133

words back.

"From this time forward, I'll be totally focused on the case. Abbey and Jessie left this evening for Florida."

"I know Pinecrest isn't the safest place, but by themselves?"

"No, with Ruth and Josh Morgan."

Shock flooded her system, and she couldn't think of anything to reply.

"I wouldn't have done it if I hadn't thought it was the safest way to go, but now I have every incentive to find this guy. I want my daughter and sister back as soon as possible before..." His voice trailed off, and he turned his back on her. "Which is the newest journal?"

The strain in his voice drew her to him. "Why Ruth and Josh?" *Aren't you worried what they'll say and do?* She reached around him and plucked the top diary from the taller stack. "I never thought you would do something like that."

He took the journal from her. "When it comes to Abbey and Jessie, I'll do everything I need to keep them unharmed. I know the risk I'm taking. Ruth could leave and never return with my daughter, but that would mean she's willing to cut ties with Pinecrest. Kidnapping is still a crime in our country. Her standing in the community is too important to her. She'll come back and fight me in court over the custody of Abbey. But at least my daughter and sister will be alive."

"Ruth doesn't play fair."

"I know, but if nothing else, I've got a few influential reporters who want to tell my side of the story. In the long run, she won't like that kind of negative press."

"Do you really believe that?" Marcie's mother was ruthless above all else.

"No, but I'm trying to convince myself. That's why I wasn't here an hour ago. I've been driving around. I even went to the airport and watched their jet take off. The best thing I can do is pray and believe this is God's will."

"But what if it isn't?" In the past five years, she'd had her faith shaken to its core. How was it that Gabriel hadn't?

Inhaling a deep breath, he closed his eyes for a few seconds. The bleak expression in his eyes attested to his dilemma. "I can't fight Him, too."

She covered his hand holding the bright pink book. "I need to remember that. I'm going to put some coffee on. I need caffeine if I'm reading the rest of the journals." Touching him connected her to Gabriel. They were in this together. The thought comforted her.

She waited in the kitchen while the pot percolated then filled two large mugs and returned to her living room. After setting his drink on the table next to him, she sat on the other end of the couch. Occasionally, she slid a glance toward him because she remembered the uncharitable comments Marcie had written about Gabriel, but his expression remained stoic as if he were reading about a fictional character. And perhaps he was. The man in those pages, especially the last four years of their marriage hadn't been family orientated. He'd been selfish and demeaning. But then maybe reading it with the notion he was innocent would put a different light on what was written by

Marcie. It certainly had changed her perspective on the earlier years.

Silence ruled until eleven o'clock and her doorbell chimed. Gabriel rose at the same time she did.

"That's probably a police officer," she said while making her way into the foyer. "I can take care of it. Go on and read."

"I'd feel better if I'm with you." As she looked out the peephole, Gabriel peeked out the narrow blinds on the side of the door.

When Kira faced Officer Byrd a few seconds later, she frowned. "Why are you sitting out front? I told you I was fine."

The patrolman swung his narrow-eyed gaze to Gabriel. "Chief Shaffer told me to until *he* leaves."

Gabriel stepped closer to Kira until their arms brushed against each other. "So you can follow me home?"

She clasped his hand. "If you want to sit in your car out front, fine but don't ring the doorbell every hour. We're working."

"Yes, ma'am. But if you need me, I'll be here." The officer threw a last glance at

Gabriel as Kira shut the door.

"If looks could kill..." He headed for the living room.

Kira followed him. "Bill and Officer Byrd are tight, and Bill hates to be wrong. He feels your release is a black mark against him. Your walking around is evidence for the whole town that our police chief made a mistake."

Gabriel settled in the same spot on the couch and picked up the journal he was reading. His hands gripped its sides.

"I'm sorry you have to read what she wrote about you."

"Things were bad between us the last few years, but I never realized the depth of her feelings against me." He flipped back several pages and pointed at it. "This is the second discrepancy I've found."

Kira scooted next to him. "What?"

"She makes it sound like she was at the ranch. I know she wasn't that day and night. I knew she didn't want to live there, but I couldn't afford to have a house in town, too. So when she periodically went to visit a girlfriend who lives in Oklahoma City overnight, I was relieved. This was one of those times."

"Who? I was in town by this time. She never said anything to me."

"Hannah Waters. She moved away before you came back to Pinecrest."

"Why wouldn't Marcie just say that?"

"Because it was a lie. If she was having an affair as she told me, then that must have been when."

"Did you ever talk to Hannah?"

"If I needed Marcie, I called her on her cell phone. I don't have Hannah's number, and I saw no point in contacting her after Marcie let me know she had an affair."

"I'm going to get in touch with Hannah. We need to know who Marcie had an affair with. She might know, especially if Marcie saw him while in Oklahoma City."

As the hours passed, Kira read the later diaries, noting each time Marcie went out of town, often to Oklahoma City. In the latter entries, there were even more subtle changes in her childhood friend, more bitterness and anger. When she finished the last journal, her eyes burned and a deep weariness cloaked her. She checked her watch: 7:00 a.m. Where had the time gone?

Kira glanced at Gabriel, engrossed in the pages before him. His stack of unread diaries had shrunk to three. She rose and grabbed their mugs. "I'll refill this."

She poured coffee into both of their cups then made a fresh pot. She paused in the entrance and watched him as he read. None of the earlier tension lined his face, but then he wasn't mentioned in her high school journals, except a couple of times at the end of Marcie senior year.

While she set his mug on the end table near him, he closed one and took another. Their gazes linked, and the anguish she glimpsed in his eyes stole her breath.

"What's wrong?" Kira took the seat next to him on the couch.

He clutched one of the journals from Marcie's freshman year. "I wish I'd read these years ago. So much has been explained about her in these pages. Her desperate need to be loved. Her need to be validated. Now I realize I never really knew the woman I married. I thought I had at one time." Gabriel surged to his feet and prowled the living room. "I have to find this murderer. Ruth has Abbey. I don't want my daughter around her grandmother for long periods of time. Look at what Ruth did to Marcie. She had anything money could buy, but the one thing she wanted was acceptance and love from her mother. Ruth was incapable of giving Marcie that."

"I think you did for a while."

He halted his pacing and faced her. "But her mother was always there in the background chipping away at Marcie. Our marriage never had a chance."

Kira searched her mind for something to say that would make a difference. She couldn't.

The ringing of the doorbell sliced the air as though a guillotine swooshed down.

She jumped to her feet and headed toward the foyer, her pulse thudding through her body. "Obviously Wally doesn't understand what *don't ring my bell* means." She started to swing the door open.

Gabriel clamped her arm and stopped

141

her. "Check who it is. Don't ever assume anything."

When he released his grasp, Kira stood on tiptoes, saw who was out on the porch and sighed. After turning the lock, she pulled on the knob, backing away a couple of steps.

Chief Shaffer barged inside and peered into the living room. "Where is he?"

"Who?"

"Michaels. There's been another murder."

SIX

When Gabriel first heard the police chief's voice, he grabbed his mug and headed through the dining room into the kitchen to refill his cup with the freshly brewed coffee. After being emotionally racked over the coals by Marcie in the journals, he didn't want to deal with Bill Shaffer. He wouldn't be able to escape the man for long, but he needed a moment of private time with the Lord.

Holding the mug cupped in his hands, he leaned against the counter and bowed his head. *Give me the strength to be civil to the man, Lord. I may need his help in finding the murderer. I know I need Yours to show me who murdered those women and to keep Abbey, Jessie—and Kira—safe from the killer.*

When he opened his eyes and looked toward the entrance, Kira stood there. The pain and grief in her gaze chilled him deep into the marrow of his bones. "What happened?"

"Mary Lou Peters is missing. She left work at the grocery store at ten last night and never came home. With all that has been going on, her mother called the police this morning when she went into her room to wake her up and discovered she didn't even come home."

No! He'd just talked to her a few days ago. Mary Lou and Jessie were friends. Gabriel set his mug on the counter and covered the distance to Kira. "No chance she had a date and stayed out all night?"

"Not so far. The police are checking with all her friends."

"So why is the chief here?" *Can't he give me peace?*

Kira averted her gaze, looking over his shoulder.

"For me. He still thinks I'm the killer," Gabriel finally muttered.

"Not now. I told him you were here from ten until now reading Marcie's journals, and we have an officer who sat in his patrol car last night to back up our alibi."

"*Our* alibi?"

She clasped his upper arms. "We are in this together. I won't rest until this guy is caught. Bill is slow to change, but he will."

Her touch conveyed her support, and the idea he wasn't in this alone shored up his determination to find the killer. Gabriel wasn't sure Bill would. What had he done to create such hatred in the police chief that kept him hanging onto a wrong perception? The courts cleared him. Why wasn't that enough for Bill?

He moved past Kira and strode into the living room, his jaw locked so tightly it ached. "You think I know where Mary Lou is?"

At the window staring outside, Chief Shaffer pivoted and glared at Gabriel. "Do you know?"

"No, but let me call my buddy, the sociopath killer, and ask him."

Daggers shot out of the police chief's eyes. "Please do." His hand rested on the butt of his gun in its holster.

"Just as soon as I can figure out who he is, I will. No one wants this man in jail more than me."

The police chief studied Gabriel for a long moment. The hostility emanating from Bill lessened. "You didn't deserve Marcie. You two were so different."

Gabriel remembered how Bill had tried to date Marcie, and she'd turned him down. She made fun of the police chief being her mom's pawn, but pointing that out wouldn't do any good now. "In hindsight, I agree, but I tried to make the best of a rocky situation."

The police chief's gaze shifted to Kira standing next to Gabriel. "Have the journals helped you any?"

"We're not quite finished reading them all. I've seen a few references to a 'he' that I thought was Gabriel when I originally went through them, but now I realize it wasn't him. Reading them from a different perspective has opened my eyes to what preconceived notions can do when looking at a piece of evidence."

Bill stiffened. "Are you saying that's what I did?"

"Only you can answer that, but I did. I believed the evidence against Gabriel, and as a result, I didn't look at the journals as a way to prove he was innocent. Marcie told Gabriel she had a lover. What if that man was the murderer?"

"Then why is he killing all the other women?"

"Good question, Bill. You can ask him when we find him." Kira moved to the couch, her arm sweeping over the stack of diaries. "We'll be finished this morning, and then I'll give you an overview of what we've come up with. You should go through them with an open mind. You might be surprised how your outlook changes. I loved Marcie, but she had problems."

The weariness deep inside Gabriel abated as he listened to Kira stand up to the police chief. She *really* believed he was innocent. That was a solace he didn't realize he needed until now. "Speaking about Marcie and the journals, I didn't see one after the twentieth of December. That's three weeks before her disappearance. There should be one. Where is it?"

Kira peered at Bill. "I don't remember there being one. I just assumed it was a time gap between journals. There was another missing period not long after y'all separated."

"Yeah, I noticed that. A month. I can't answer about that gap, but when I went through her bedroom to her connected bathroom to retrieve Abbey's antibiotic she was taking, I know I saw a journal on her nightstand with a scene of lightning in a dark storm on its cover."

Again Kira and Bill exchanged looks.

The police chief scowled. "These are all we had in evidence. That we found at her house. Are you sure it isn't here?"

"I would have remembered that. She chose her next journal based on her mood at the time she started it. I even asked her what was going on. For Abbey's sake, I was concerned, but Marcie told me to stay out of her business, that I didn't have a right anymore to know what she was doing. I sent Abbey to my truck and tried once again to find out what was wrong. Marcie laughed." He still remembered how it had sounded—an eerie, hysterical ring to it. "That's when she told me she had a lover who was better than I ever was. I didn't stay around. Abbey was waiting and, frankly, I was tired of dealing with Marcie's drama."

"That means someone took it." Kira sat on the couch and went through the stacks.

Bill pinned him with a narrow-eyed gaze. "Did you look at it when you saw it?"

Tension clamped about Gabriel's chest. "No. I never read her journals."

Bill snorted. "Sure. You want us to believe you never took one little peek during those years you were married to her?"

"You can believe what you want. *I* know I didn't. Would you make a habit of reading your wife's?"

Bill closed the space between them, his

hands balled at his sides. His glare cut through him. "You're treading on shaky ground. My wife has nothing to do with this investigation, but yours does."

Technically he had still been Marcie's husband. They were separated but not divorced when she died. "If you'd listened to me when I tried to tell you I didn't murder my wife, you might not have two other dead women, and possibly Mary Lou, killed, too. I could have helped you. You never gave me a chance."

"And I'm not now!" Bill's voice rose, nearly a shout.

Kira placed herself between Bill and Gabriel but faced the police chief. "Are you going to let your pride stand in the way of finding the murderer? We now know that one, possibly two, journals are missing. That's a lead."

"How's that a lead? It doesn't tell us who the killer is unless we find the journals, which according to you two are gone. Probably destroyed by now."

"He might not have damaged them. But even if he did, it tells us that Marcie did most likely have a lover like she told Gabriel. And if not, why were they taken? She wrote something that he didn't want anyone to know."

Bill jabbed his finger in Gabriel's direction. "That describes Gabriel. They were separated. What we read wasn't flattering, so I can just imagine what Marcie said that we didn't read. He could have taken them."

Kira shook her head. "Get out. I'm not going down this route again. There's no point talking to you until you let go of your anger. It colors your judgment."

Bill opened and closed his hands then pivoted and stalked to the door. It slammed so hard a couple of pictures on the wall in the foyer shook.

Kira slowly rotated toward Gabriel. "I'll talk to him later when he cools down. The killer is escalating. If I have to run a separate investigation, I will. I'm going to talk to the sheriff about utilizing a few deputies to help if I need it."

"I wish now I had read what was in her journals. Then maybe we wouldn't have women being murdered in Pinecrest." Gabriel sank onto the couch and reclined, his head resting on the back cushion. "I still have two more to read. I want to finish. Then we can talk. After that honestly, I never want to see these journals again."

Kira sat next to him and laid her hand over his, the warmth of her touch a gentle reminder she was on his side now. "I can't imagine what you're going through reading all of these."

"I wish Marcie had talked to me rather than write everything in a journal. I saw a time where we could have made it if she'd shared her feelings, especially concerning her mother. That woman did a number on her daughter. I don't want Abbey to ever see these. After we catch the killer, I want to burn every one of them."

"I'll see that it's done. If Ruth Morgan read these, she would agree. This doesn't paint her in a good light." Kira squeezed his hand then rose. "While you're reading, I'll fix some scrambled eggs and toast for breakfast."

When Kira left the room, Gabriel pushed

forward and grabbed one of Marcie's freshman year journals. It was worse reading these older journals from high school, especially her sophomore and freshman years, than reviewing the ones written during their marriage. Ruth had an ironclad hold on her daughter. Marcie was to fit into a certain mold, and Ruth wasn't going to accept anything less. Any anger he'd felt toward his deceased wife was gone. She might have come from a wealthy family, but at least he'd grown up knowing how much his mother had loved him no matter what.

There's a dance at school. Craig asked me to go with him. I didn't really want to, but if Mom had let me, I would have. I'd thought she would be happy with him. His dad is a doctor. But she told me no one in Pinecrest was acceptable. I can't even go with my girlfriends.

That had been one of many entries in the journals where Marcie tried to fit in at school, but her mother wouldn't let her. She couldn't join any clubs or play sports. Ruth had only let her be part of the church youth group. By her sophomore year, she'd begun to count down the days until she was eighteen. Not long after she turned that age, Marcie had started dating him.

Gabriel sighed and forced himself to read the rest. Then he never wanted to again—even for the case.

* * *

Later that afternoon in her office, the words on the pages began to blur together for Kira. Gabriel wasn't picking her up for another half an hour, and she'd run out of steam. At least tonight she shouldn't have any trouble falling asleep. She used her folded arms on her desk as a pillow while she laid her head on them and closed her eyes.

But her mind wouldn't shut down. She kept thinking about different passages from Marcie's journals. *He was rough today. I kinda liked it.*

Who was he? This morning, Gabriel said that was one of the passages that didn't refer to him. It had been written right after she'd come home from visiting her friend in Oklahoma City. Kira had to leave a message on Hannah Waters' voicemail, asking her to call as soon as possible. She hoped Hannah could help the investigation.

I let him tie me up. It was exciting. He's different. Not anything like I thought.

When she and Gabriel had discussed that entry at breakfast, his hurt tangled with his anger. The more they talked about the journals, the more they decided the mysterious "he" was the most likely candidate for the killer. Last winter when she'd read those passages, she'd assumed it was Gabriel, and the behavior hadn't surprised her because she was sure he was the murderer.

Her new perception of what was written in the journals changed the list of suspects from one man to all the other men in the area. Although for Marcie to be involved with him, the suspect had to be a certain type. The problem was Kira hadn't known her friend as well as she'd thought. What type of man had Marcie liked? When Marcie turned eighteen, she dated whoever was forbidden before she'd become a legal adult and had inherited her grandmother's trust money—enough to live on her own.

A knock at the door sounded.

Kira lifted her head. "Come in."

Bill entered her office, tired lines grooved deep into his tanned face. He took a seat in front of her desk, removing his Stetson and laying it on the empty chair next to him. "We went back to the original burial site of the first three women and looked for a fresh grave. We worked out from there and didn't find anything. I even used a cadaver dog. I let it sniff one of Mary Lou's jackets. Nothing. No one has seen her. Her car was found abandoned on Tyler Road."

"Any evidence of foul play?"

"No. Her car wouldn't start. It must have stalled. We canvassed that area, too. No sign of her, and no one saw her."

"I've been thinking about the victims. I figured out one thing everyone had in common besides going to Pinecrest High School."

Bill sat forward. "What?"

"We were all members of the youth group for teenagers at Pinecrest Community Church. That leaves an age range of five to six years. Even Mary Lou fits in although she is younger than Marcie, Shirley, and Rebecca."

"Okay." A doubtful look clouded his eyes. "I'll stop by and see the pastor. He might have a list of people from the youth group back then. I've requested help from the state police. One of them is already here, and a couple more are coming in tomorrow. We'll be widening our search for Mary Lou. Larry will be assigned to you during the daytime. Wally will take over at night. That's all I can spare."

"If you need either one or both for the search, Gabriel is—"

"No, the killer has already come after you once at *his* ranch."

Kira rose. "I know I was part of that youth group with the others. I'll try to remember everyone who was in it in case Pastor Dunkin can't find a list of members. At its height it had up to twenty-five teenagers."

"Are you listening to me about Gabriel? He isn't to be trusted."

She came from around behind her desk and crossed to the window overlooking Main Street. Gabriel pulled into a parking space in front of the courthouse. He was probably more exhausted than she was because he had to go home and work at the ranch with Hank. As he headed toward the building, his strides were shorter, slower. Maybe she should avail herself of the two police officers not because of Bill and his opinion, but because Gabriel needed to run his ranch and get some rest. They could still work on the case together in the evenings. She'd been fine today with Larry on duty in the reception area of her office.

"I'm fine with those two officers, but what I do on my time isn't to be questioned by you or them. We discovered information last night that may help in finding the killer, especially if we find who Marcie was seeing at that time." She turned away from the window as Gabriel disappeared inside the courthouse.

"You're not an investigator. You're a prosecutor. Do your job, and I'll do mine." Bill surged to his feet and left her office.

She hoped Gabriel and Bill missed each other in the hall, but when Gabriel arrived in her office, his stoic expression and rigid set of his shoulders told her otherwise.

He shut the door so Larry and Penny in the outer office didn't hear their conversation. "The police chief crossed the lobby so he could let me know he would have an officer available to guard you 24/7. He's using two right now, but after the search for Mary Lou ends, there will be another one. He wasn't too happy when I asked who would protect all the other females in Pinecrest who were between the ages of twenty-five to forty years old."

"You didn't?" She was surprised she hadn't heard Bill shouting at Gabriel from two floors away.

He cocked a grin and pushed his cowboy hat back. "Well, not exactly but I was thinking it. I'm already on the bad side of our police chief. I think I know why Bill is so mad at me. He wanted to be the one who married Marcie. He has a wife now, but not until five years ago. He's a few years older than Marcie, but even when she was a teenager, he was always around her, doing her biding. Not just Ruth's."

"Marcie had a lot of guys 'in love' with her. She was the unattainable gal everyone wanted."

He blew out a long breath. "If only they had known…"

How many times had he regretted marrying Marcie?

"I hope you're hungry, because I'm fixing dinner tonight. But first you have to take me by the grocery store. I need a few supplies." Kira grabbed her purse and coat while Gabriel opened the door. When she spied Larry, she told him her plans, then left with Gabriel, aware the officer trailed them.

As she shopped, she tried to forget the last time she'd been there. Mary Lou had been alive, and Kira had come face to face with Gabriel after his release. Now she actually was looking forward to cooking for him. She enjoyed trying different recipes, but tonight she planned something simple and delicious. A man's meal—steak, baked potatoes, and green beans with a slice of Grams' peach cobbler.

By the time she sat catty-cornered from Gabriel at her kitchen table two hours later, she'd be happy if she could make it through the meal without falling asleep. Even drinking a caffeine-charged drink wasn't doing much to help keep her awake.

Kira played with her baked potato. "My brain feels like this. Crumbling into pieces, but I do think we've made some progress in the investigation."

Gabriel put his forefinger against his lips and said, "Shh. Larry might hear, or is Wally here now?"

In spite of her weariness, she laughed. "Larry had his chance to eat dinner with us."

"But Wally was relieving him at seven."

"I should have asked Wally if he wanted to join us."

"And give him a heart attack after your exchange with him last night. He wasn't too happy with either of us. He feels my presence at your house was the reason he was stuck outside yesterday, and now he gets to do it over. At least he doesn't have to worry that I'm killing you. Are you sure you don't want me to stay?"

"What I want is my life back. I don't like people watching over me. We both need a good night's sleep. I hope to go to Oklahoma City and interview Hannah. Anything she can tell us about this mysterious lover will help. I thought we could go tomorrow afternoon. I know you need time to work at your ranch, so if you can't, I'm dragging Larry along with me."

"Poor guy. I'll go with you instead. Give him some time off."

"If Bill doesn't insist he accompany us."

Kira tried to stifle a yawn but couldn't. "I'd rather Larry join in the search for Mary Lou."

"Have you ever wondered why the killer has contacted you?"

"Every day. I have a feeling I know him, but then if it is someone in Pinecrest, I know a lot of men who live here so that doesn't narrow the list down." Kira finally took a bite of her baked potato and washed it down with a swig of lukewarm coffee. "I'm finding myself suspecting all the men—even the ones I've known a long time. What if it's somehow connected to the youth group I was part of?"

Gabriel's forehead furrowed. "You think a guy that was in the group with you is the killer?"

"Maybe, but it could just as well be someone who was on the outside." Kira shook her head. "I don't know what to think anymore. The males in the group were people like Al, Craig, Larry, my mechanic, Jeremy, the mayor, my secretary's nephew, as well as Josh. He was there to keep an eye on his younger sister. Marcie used to complain all the time about that." Who was she leaving out? "Oh, and even Kenny was for a short time. I see him every day at the courthouse." She scooped up green beans, cold now, and ate them. "Why weren't you in the youth group? Jessie was."

"I was mad at God. My dad left us. One day he was there, the next gone. He didn't even leave a note."

"You never heard from him again?"

"Yes, when his lawyer contacted my mother for a divorce."

"I begged God to change my dad's mind. My mother's health was going downhill. She pined for him."

"And then you were found guilty of a crime you didn't commit."

"Yeah, but that is actually what brought me back to the Lord. I don't think I'd have made it in prison without Him. He gave me the strength to wake up each day and hope people would discover the truth that I didn't kill Marcie."

"And He answered your prayer."

"I think He answered my prayer the first time. We were better off without my father. I just didn't know it at that time."

All this talk about fathers prodded Kira's memories. Her mother divorced, returned to Pinecrest, and lived with Grams. Dad sent a birthday card and a Christmas gift every year, but that was all. "I didn't know mine at all. He divorced my mom when I was three. I don't have any memories of him."

It was Gabriel's turn to reach out and clasp her hand. "I didn't want that for my marriage. I hung on as long as I could. Being a father is the most important job I have. Abbey means everything to me. I'm not going to let Ruth ruin her life like she did Marcie's. If I have to sell the ranch to fight Ruth, I will."

"You have me on your side. There's got to be a way to keep this from becoming a battle between you and Ruth."

"I hope so. I don't want to hurt Abbey in the process."

Through the weariness pressing down on Kira, she smiled at Gabriel, cupping her hand over his. "Abbey is lucky to have you as her dad."

His smoldering look sent a shiver down her spine. Her eyelids slid halfway closed. She wished they weren't in the middle of a murder case. She wished she'd never prosecuted him in the first place. She wished she believed in marriage and happily ever after.

She slipped her arm away before she

succumbed to the newfound sensations rampaging through her. He could make her forget her ex-husband's domineering and demeaning behavior. To believe not all men were like Jonathan and her father.

As much as she wished she could spend time with Gabriel without the case standing between them and talking about something that wasn't about the murders, sleepiness nipped at her. She yawned.

He grinned. "Go to bed, Kira. I'll clean up then make sure everything is locked before I leave."

As she pushed to her feet, he did, too. "I'll call you tomorrow about the trip to see Hannah." She leaned toward him and kissed him on the cheek. "Good night."

She headed for her bedroom, paused, and glanced back. He stacked the dishes on the kitchen table, stopped, and peered at her. His smile reached deep inside her and gave her hope that at least one day he would forgive her for her part in his imprisonment.

She turned away and walked to her bedroom. One look at her bed, and she made her way to it, set the alarm on her cell phone, and put it on the nightstand then laid down, not even taking time to undress. Sleep descended quickly, whisking her into blackness...

Through the dark, a persistent ringing sounded, pulling her awake. She didn't want to leave the comfort of nothingness, but the noise started grating against her nerves. She blinked her eyes open and fumbled for her nearby phone.

As she brought it to her, she pushed the accept button and cupped it to her ear, murmuring, "Hello."

"You're looking in the wrong place for Mary Lou," a mechanical voice said.

"Where?" Kira struggled to sit up.

"Jessie knows where they used to love spending time in the summer. Stop me."

SEVEN

Gabriel stared at the pond on the south section of his ranch. The frigid wind from the north pierced through his heavy coat and buried deep into him. If his sister had been in town, this could have been Jessie the authorities were searching for. Instead the divers were scouring the cold waters for her best friend. This was the last place Jessie could think of that she and Mary Lou had spent their time in the summer, especially the past one when he'd been in prison.

A diver popped up to the surface. "Found a body."

Gabriel squeezed his eyes closed. *Why*

here, Lord?

Kira grasped his gloved hand. "Why did he change his MO?"

The physical link to Kira, her familiar scent of lilacs, and the soft sound of her voice warmed Gabriel in spite of the cold wind. "More importantly, why did he dump the body here? Why did he contact you last night? As much as I wish this were a stranger passing through town, it isn't. It's someone who knows you. Maybe even watching your house. He called you not five minutes after I left."

"When he said 'stop me' at the end, it was different." She shuddered.

"How?"

"There was a time I thought the words stop me was a desperate plea, but I'm not sure it wasn't a challenge instead."

Ignoring the police chief staring at him as if he were guilty, Gabriel released her hand and slipped his arm around her shoulders then pressed her against him. "We're going to get him. Mary Lou will be his last victim. I'm staying with you at all times. I don't care what the police chief says or does. Hank can take care of what absolutely needs to be done at the ranch. The rest will have to wait."

"You think I'm next."

"I'm not taking the chance. He's fixated on you in a different way, but that could change in an instant."

As Mary Lou's body was carried from the pond, Hank joined Gabriel and Kira, "This is where Jessie came with Mary Lou to get away from all the things happening in town and at the ranch. They met here every hot afternoon to swim and talk. How did she take it when you told her Mary Lou was missing and might be the next victim?"

His sister's sobs resounded in his mind. "She wants to come home and help track down this maniac."

Hank squinted against the glare of the sun. "That's Jessie for you."

"When I tell her we found Mary Lou's body, I don't know how much longer she'll stay in Florida. All she'll want to do is get her hands on the killer. When I talked to her last, she did tell me that Josh ended up coming back to Pinecrest two days ago."

"Josh?" Kira glanced at him. "I haven't heard anything about him being here. You'd think he'd be on the police chief's case and making a lot of noise because there's a fourth victim."

"This is my cue to leave. Chief Shaffer is heading this way. We've exchanged a lot of uncivilized words this past year," Hank said and mounted the gelding he'd ridden to the pond.

Gabriel bent close to Kira's ear. "Can we escape, too?"

"We will, now that the body has been discovered. We have a date in Oklahoma City with Hannah. Let me do the talking with the chief."

"Worried he'll haul me to jail again for saying what I think?"

"Shh."

Bill planted himself in front of Gabriel. "If you didn't have an ironclad alibi, I'd be hauling you to jail."

"Yeah, I'd be stupid enough to dispose of a dead body on my own land. Bill, give me more credit than that."

Kira poked her elbow into his side.

"We're leaving right now for Oklahoma City. We should be back late tonight. I can call the station when we return to Pinecrest. Then Wally can meet us at my house."

"Oklahoma City? Why?"

"I want to talk to Hannah Waters about Marcie's visits to see her."

"You think the killer was the guy who Marcie went to see in Oklahoma City? If so, why did he wait so long to murder her?" Bill peered over his shoulder as the van with the body drove away.

"Even if he isn't the killer, but only her former lover, he may know something. It's worth the trip. Do you have a better lead?"

"Not at the moment, but I'll have Mary Lou's body autopsied right away. Maybe there will be a clue on it. She's only been dead a couple of days. The others were much longer before we found them."

"Don't get your hopes up, Bill. The killer called me because he wanted us to find Mary Lou. He's still in control."

The police chief snorted, his mouth firmed in a frown. "You can take Larry if you want."

Gabriel gritted his teeth together to bite back the words, "No, thanks. Larry is the newest officer on the force."

"No one knows where we're going. This killer has struck in both the daytime and nighttime. Another officer out on the streets patrolling is a good use of Larry." Kira inched closer to Gabriel as though to present a united front.

Finally Gabriel said, "I'll make sure no one follows us out of town. We'll call Hannah when we arrive in the city. I won't let anything happen to Kira."

As Gabriel and Kira strode toward his truck, the police chief said, "Remember the killer is in control."

Gabriel stopped, tensing.

"Keep walking. That's why Bill is so mad. He likes to be in control, and he isn't." Kira's whispered words eased the anger mounting in Gabriel.

"How have you managed to work with him all these years?"

"Unlike some men, Bill is easy to read and, therefore, it's easy to get him to do what I want."

Gabriel chuckled. "How much will you pay me to keep that to myself?"

"I'll buy dinner tonight." She gave him a smile.

"Well then we need to go to the fanciest restaurant in Oklahoma City."

* * *

Sitting in Hannah's living room, Kira shared a look with Gabriel. "Are you sure the guy she was seeing when she came to visit you lived in the Oklahoma City area?"

"Yes, that's what Marcie indicated to me. She said he worked long hours so she had to come to him."

"Did he pick her up here?" Kira hoped they could get a make of his car.

"Never. He'd call her, and she'd leave right after that."

Gabriel leaned forward, resting his elbows on his thighs. "He called her on her cell phone?"

"A cell phone but it wasn't her regular one. That's one of the things she loved about seeing him. Everything was secretive and a bit dangerous."

Kira slid a glance to Gabriel, his face like a sculpture in granite. "What do you mean dangerous?"

"I'm not...comfortable talking about it sitting in front of her husband." Hannah dropped her gaze to a spot on the floor between them.

"I can leave if you want, but nothing you say will surprise me about Marcie. Our marriage had really been over for a few years before we started the divorce proceedings. I tried to keep it together for Abbey's sake."

Hannah cleared her throat. "I didn't know you well in school, but toward the end I didn't like what Marcie was doing. I finally told her I wouldn't be part of what she was doing."

"When was the last time she came to visit you?" According to the journal, her trips out of town continued until a month before she died.

"Two years ago." Hannah shifted her attention to Gabriel. "The reason I think the man was dangerous was I saw bruises on her that developed after she saw him. The time I told her not to come back she'd been crying in my guest bedroom. Instead of getting mad at the man, she got mad at me. I couldn't stand by and watch her self-destruct."

He lowered his head and kneaded his nape. "You said the phone wasn't her regular one. What was it?"

"A burner phone she would toss away once she returned to Pinecrest. That was one of the things she liked about meeting him. She told me all the intrigue added spice to her dull life."

Gabriel winced. "She loved going for the forbidden. If she'd been told she couldn't fly, she would have tried anyway."

If Marcie had come to Oklahoma City some time last year, Kira could track her movements through the GPS on her phone. Marcie's was in the evidence room in a box where they stored the solved crimes. "Did she take her cell or the burner one with her when she went to meet him?"

"She always left her cell phone here."

Although disappointed Marcie hadn't taken her regular cell phone with her, the idea of tracking with GPS spurred another idea. She shifted toward Gabriel. "I wonder about the GPS on the new car she got last year. Maybe that could tell us where she went at least."

"You need to talk to Ruth about that. She bought the sports car for Marcie's birthday as a reward for finally wanting to divorce me."

"If Josh is in town, I'll go out to the estate and talk with him. He would know." Finally a lead she could follow.

Gabriel frowned. "Not without me. I don't trust him."

Tension vibrated between them. She remembered the black eye he gave Josh. She hoped she wouldn't have to be a referee between them. "Fine. We can go tomorrow."

"I'll be on my best behavior," he said as though he could read her thoughts.

Kira turned to Hannah, sitting in a chair opposite her. "Anything else?"

The woman chewed on her bottom lip.

"Nothing I can think of, but if I come up with something that might help, I'll give you a call."

Kira rose at the same time Gabriel did. "Thank you. Call me any time. That's my cell phone number I gave you earlier."

Hannah showed them to the front door. "I knew Marcie was using me, but I got the feeling her lover was using her. After seeing him, she would always be so subdued. I wish I knew more."

Kira hugged Hannah. "Thanks for trying to help. If you ever come back to Pinecrest, let me know. We can have lunch."

Gabriel shook the woman's hand then stepped out onto the porch.

The chill in the air hinted at a possible chance of snow. "I'm glad we ate before coming here. I know the weatherman only said we had a twenty percent possibility of bad weather, but that's usually when we get it for sure."

"Yeah, we have a two hour drive." Gabriel escorted her to the passenger side and opened the door.

As she settled herself in the seat, he

hurried around the front and climbed inside. She shivered. "Too bad you don't have one of those vehicles you can start from the comfort of a warm house and turn on the heater."

"It doesn't take long. Set it on whatever you want." Gabriel backed out of the driveway. "Do you think Hannah is telling us everything?"

"Yes. Why wouldn't she?"

"In Marcie's journals, *he* appeared after Hannah told her not to come back. She was gone at least once every six or eight weeks to 'see Hannah.' After we separated, she was going out of town every other weekend."

"So she never met him in Pinecrest. What if he isn't from our town? What if he isn't the killer? I can't see the lover coming all the way to Pinecrest to kill our four victims. Marcie, yes, but not the others. If he planned to murder women, wouldn't he do it closer to home? A stranger would be noticed after a time or two."

Gabriel pulled onto the two-lane highway heading to Pinecrest. "Has the chief checked on similar murders in the Oklahoma City area?"

"He did when the three women were found. No similar burials or kill method like the ones in Pinecrest have been done in the state. I'll make sure Bill expands to other states."

"How about murders where the victims were disposed of in a body of water? Or unsolved serial killings?"

"I'll see what I can get. He started a pattern with the first three, but with Mary Lou, he changed it. I'd like to know why?"

"Don't know. The police did find his burial site. Maybe that was it. I'm having a hard time thinking like a sociopath. What drives a person to kill for fun?"

"Control, the feeling of power they have over another. Sometimes the reason is hard for a normal person to grasp."

The oncoming headlights illuminated the hard planes of Gabriel's face. "Having no control or power was what drove Marcie to rebel against her mother. How could she willingly go from Ruth to a man who dominated her? What Hannah said to us describes a dominant partner in the relationship. She never indicated to me..."

Kira glanced at Gabriel. "What?"

"I just remembered when we first married that Marcie wanted me to tie her to the bed. Then another time she taunted me, trying to get me to slap her. When I told her no, she backed off, but my answer had surprised her."

"Your reputation in high school and afterwards was a 'bad boy' one. Maybe she thought you liked playing rough." Kira shook her head, even more shocked at how much she hadn't known about Marcie. "She should have married my ex-husband instead."

"Why? Did he hit you?"

"Not at first but he was always controlling. Again I didn't see that while we were dating, but not long after we were married, if I didn't comply with what he wanted to do, he would tear me down emotionally. I began to think something was really wrong with me. I could never please Jonathan. Finally when he hit me so hard, I fell down the staircase, cracking some ribs. That was the final straw. I left him so quickly, his head spun." The memory of his anger and threats still caused her heart to race. "I'm beginning to feel I'm not good at reading people." As a lawyer, she had thought she could read body language and discover what people felt but didn't say. She realized she'd honed her skills over the past few years. She'd known Marcie wasn't the same girl from high school, but that didn't mean she was going to give up on their friendship. She married Jonathan while a senior in college. She had been starry eyed and naïve. That changed as an assistant DA in Tulsa and Pinecrest.

"Sometimes we have to just put our trust in the Lord. I learned that the hard way. I didn't have any control over going to prison. Nothing I said made a difference. Everyone thought I was the killer, especially since some of the evidence could be taken that way. What I said was considered a lie. I reached the bottom of a dark pit when my mother died. Finally, I gave it all to God. He was responsible for that couple hiking with their German shepherd and finding one of the graves in the woods."

"Do you ever question God?"

"Yes. When I sent Abbey and Jessie away. When Mary Lou was murdered. But getting Jessie out of town might have saved her life. The killer could have taken her instead of Mary Lou. They were often together. I don't know what the future holds, but evil will be around us as long as we're alive. It's part of this world. What we can control is how we deal with it."

"And I intend to find this man and see him answer for his crimes."

"Not without my help," Gabriel said in the silence that hung in the air. "We are in this together. Promise me you won't try to do this alone."

Warmth flowed through her at his fervent tone. She never had the sense they were a team with Jonathan. Although married, she'd always felt alone. Was that the way Gabriel had felt about Marcie? For years, Kira had thought she and Gabriel had nothing in common, but that had been

Marcie's conception of him, not the man Kira had been working with.

Near the outskirts of Pinecrest, she glanced at the dashboard clock. Almost midnight. She gave the police station a call and told the dispatcher that she would be at her house in fifteen minutes so the woman would notify Wally.

In the distance, the lights of town shone as though a beacon. Snow flurries, coming down faster, smashed against the windshield.

"I hope we don't get a lot of bad weather," she said as more landed on the glass and melted.

"Abbey loves the first snowfall of the year. She won't be happy she missed it."

"Whereas, I don't look forward to any during the winter. I have to drive on it, and I've never mastered the art."

"The key is to take it—"

Something hit the windshield at the same time a sound like the backfire of a truck blasted the air.

EIGHT

"Get down!" Gabriel shouted as he floored the accelerator, his truck fishtailing on the slippery road.

Adrenaline surged through him, followed by fury.

He chanced a glance at Kira to make sure she was down and all right. Another shot pierced the back window and lodged in his dashboard, missing him by a few inches.

"Are you okay?" His hands tightened about the steering wheel while he kept increasing his speed in the gentle snowfall.

"Yes. You?" Her voice quavered.

"Okay," he said between clenched teeth

as the right side of the top of his arm began to protest.

He shut down the pain easing into his consciousness. No time for it—if he wanted to remain alive. He'd like to stay and fight, but he wouldn't risk getting Kira killed. "My gun is in the glove compartment. Get it out and call 9-1-1."

A third bullet struck the cab of the truck. He prayed he was putting distance between them and the shooter. That was their only chance—making it to the lights of Pinecrest. A few, long miles away.

"We've been shot at about ten miles out of town near the Baker's ranch." Kira paused as if listening to the person on the other end. "Three. We're almost to the city limits." Another pause. "Just a minute," then Kira asked Gabriel, "Are we being followed?"

He checked the rearview window. "No lights behind us." Although that didn't mean someone wasn't following them. In the pitch dark, a car without lights could get close before he noticed it.

"Okay. We will." Kira disconnected. "Bill

said to head for the police station. He has three patrol cars coming toward us. One will escort us the rest of the way while the other two search the area where it started."

After several tense minutes, headlights and flashing red lights came toward them on the opposite side of the highway. The cavalry. He finally took a decent breath since the first shot. Pain inched into his mind as the last patrol car turned and began trailing him. When he entered the outskirts of Pinecrest, he let up on his speed and eased the tight grip on the steering wheel.

"I think you can get up now." He glanced at Kira huddling on the floor in front of her seat.

As more lights illuminated the truck interior, she gasped. "You've been shot. Your arm is bleeding."

"Just a scratch."

"Don't play the macho man. I'm letting Bill know we're heading to the hospital instead. I don't want any arguing on your part." Beneath the iron-soaked words there was a hint of a quaver.

He made a right on Main Street and drove toward Pinecrest Hospital. If he didn't, he could see Kira trying to wrestle the steering wheel from him, and in that moment, he didn't have the energy to fight both her and the pain. Maybe his graze was a little more than he thought. He slid a look at his arm. Blood drenched his shirt.

"Pull up to the emergency room. I'll have the officer move your truck." Kira placed another call to the police chief.

Lightheaded, he spied the entrance he needed and made a slight course correction. He'd almost missed the turn. As he threw the truck into park, he sighed. Between the loss of blood and his lack of sleep, his vision blurred, and he wasn't sure he could walk into the emergency room.

Before he moved to open his door, Kira was out of the truck and rounding the front. She helped him out with the officer's assistance. He heard her talking to Wally, but the words tumbled around in his mind like a tennis shoe in a dryer. An orderly met them halfway across the reception area with a wheelchair.

Gabriel collapsed in it, slumping to the side.

* * *

"Thanks, Penny. I'll see you in an hour when I get back from talking to Josh about Marcie's car." Kira punched the off button, slid her cell phone into her pocket, and left her bedroom.

As she passed her guest room, she peered at the closed door. After spending hours at the hospital while Gabriel had his gunshot wound taken care of, she hoped never to see that place again. Twice in a week was over her quota for the year. But at least Gabriel would be all right—just in pain and weak from the blood loss. It hadn't been a graze as he thought but the bullet had lodged in the fleshy part of his upper arm, having nicked a few blood vessels. It came from the same gun used on her at his ranch—the murder weapon.

When she entered her living room, Larry stood. "I want you to stay here. I'm going to Josh Morgan then right back."

"My orders are to stay with you, ma'am."

"Someone tried to kill Gabriel last night."

"You don't know that for sure. Chief Shaffer thinks the shooter was going after you again."

"Then why were all the bullets on the left side of the truck?" She hated not having freedom to go where she needed for her job. Her life and Gabriel's were on the line, not to mention other women in the town.

"You'll have to take that up with the chief."

"No, she doesn't." Gabriel stood in the entrance to the living room, his face pale, his feet bare, and dressed in jeans and T-shirt, part of his bandage visible. "I'm coming with you, Kira. You are not going alone to the estate."

"You're supposed to rest."

"I did. I got four hours." The resolve carved into his features, the force behind his gaze declared his intentions.

"Fine, so long as you stay in the car with Larry." She pressed her mouth into a firm line, hoping to convey her resolve.

Gabriel exchanged a look with the police officer then nodded. "I'll get my shirt and boots on and be right back."

Five minutes later, Larry drove Kira and Gabriel in the direction of the Morgan Estate, both of them sitting in the back of his patrol car.

"Never wanted to be in one of these again," Gabriel mumbled as Larry backed out of the driveway.

At least Gabriel would be safe. "Although it's Saturday, my secretary is coming over, and I'm going to work from home for a while until I have to be in court for a case on Monday. I called Hank this morning and told him what happened. He wanted you to know he'll take care of everything at the ranch. Not to worry."

"In other words, you want me to stay with you and the police officer assigned to you because you're afraid the murderer will try to kill me again."

She grinned. "No one has accused me

of being subtle."

"Did they find any evidence of the shooter?"

"Footprints in the light snow which have melted by now. They took pictures last night."

"Where did they go?"

"To a side road that led to the Miller's house. With the gravel there wasn't a usable tire print."

"What size was the shoe?"

"Boot and about a man's twelve."

"So how did this guy know we were going to be there at that time?"

"Good question. Bill is investigating it. At least there's a little evidence to follow."

"If we catch someone and can match a print to them. Boots are worn by a lot of men in Pinecrest."

"I hope Josh knows about Marcie's car." Needles of pain stabbed her neck and upper back. She was wound so tight she felt she would snap in two.

"Last night proved that we must be doing something right. Why else come after me? It doesn't fit with the rest of what the killer is doing."

Kira tried to relax. She ached from being so tense the past twelve hours, and she wasn't looking forward to talking to Josh. There was no love lost between him and his sister. As Josh and Marcie grew up, their relationship deteriorated until it was almost non-existent by the time Kira returned to Pinecrest. But once, when she was young, there had been a time she thought of Josh as an older brother.

Larry pulled up to the Morgan mansion and parked in the circular drive. When she opened her back door, the police officer climbed from the driver's seat.

Over the top of the car, she said, "I'm doing this by myself. I don't want him to think this is an interrogation." When Gabriel exited the patrol car, Kira glared at him. "You and Josh don't get along. I don't want to break up a fight between you two."

Gabriel smiled. "I'll be on my best behavior, but I *am* coming. There's a chance I wasn't the target last night." He rotated toward Larry. "If I go, will you stay out here on the porch?"

"Yes. I can do that."

Kira rolled her eyes and shook her head. "Fine. Let's go. Penny will be at my house soon."

Before she had a chance to ring the bell, the door swung open. Josh, all six feet six inches, filled the entrance. He had a hand towel slung around his neck and workout clothes on.

"It took y'all long enough to decide whether you were going to come in or not."

Although Gabriel hadn't said anything, Kira slid a glance at him. Barely concealed contempt shaped his features into a solemn frown with a tic jerking his jawline.

"Is Marcie's car here?" Kira asked hurriedly.

"Yes."

"May we see it?"

"The police searched it last January. They didn't find anything to tie to Marcie's murder so why the interest now?"

"We've discovered Marcie had a lover. We need to rule him out as a suspect. Marcie went to a lot of trouble to keep his identity a secret."

"Did the other victims have a lover, too?"

When Josh asked a question she hadn't considered yet, Kira was caught off guard. She couldn't think of anything to say for a moment.

"The police are investigating all possible connections between the four victims," Gabriel said in a calm voice.

"If we can identify Marcie's lover, then connecting the others to him will be easier." Kira's cheeks burned with embarrassment.

"I don't see how my sister's car will tell you anything. All personal items have been removed."

"So you sold it?" She wasn't a detective, but that wasn't going to stop her from looking into the case. She wanted her life back.

"No, it's here in the garage. Mom couldn't part with it. She gave it to Marcie. She was trying to bribe her to come live here again so Mom could see Abbey more. It didn't work, but my mother was positive it would once Marcie ran out of her inheritance from our grandmother. Follow me." Josh glowered at Gabriel. "You stay here. I'm not the killer or the shooter from last night."

Before Gabriel replied to Josh's silent challenge, Kira said, "I trust Josh. I'll be fifty yards away."

"Jessie told me that Gabriel was helping you, but I didn't believe it until I saw it for myself. He wasn't good for Marcie."

Marcie hadn't been good for Gabriel. But Kira kept that to herself. "He came to my recuse when someone shot at my car." Although at the time she hadn't thought the killer was after her or she'd probably be dead, but after last night she couldn't say that anymore. A few more inches to the left and Gabriel would have been hurt enough that he might have lost control of his truck. Was that the shooter's point? Had he planned to take her from the wreck?

"Isn't he such a good knight in shining armor?"

Kira stopped and frowned. "Josh, you didn't use to be this bitter and critical. What happened?"

"My sister was murdered, and as far as I'm concerned, Gabriel had the best reason to kill her."

"He didn't do it, and he was with me when the fourth victim was taken. Not to mention in jail for the second and third one."

"Then a partner could have helped him."

"Do you really think Gabriel would work with a partner in something like what's going on here?"

Josh shook his head and opened the door to the four-car garage. "Marcie's sports car is the last one."

"How are Jessie and Abbey doing?"

"Okay. Both miss Pinecrest, but Abbey loves the beach. After she does her schoolwork, she and Jessie spend a lot of time out there. Mom hired three bodyguards to keep the compound safe. I'm leaving tomorrow to fly back to Florida. We'll be celebrating Christmas there in a couple of weeks."

While we might be holed up in our houses, afraid to leave because of the killer terrorizing Pinecrest. "That's nice. Grams and I are going to have a quiet one at her house."

Josh gestured toward the red sports car. "So what will this tell you?"

Kira swung the passenger side door open and peeked inside. "What navigation and communication system did she have?"

"StarPoint. Are you going to try to get the records of her movements from them?"

"Yes. I can get a warrant, or you can persuade your mother to give us permission. If we know her movements, maybe we can figure out who her lover was. Will you ask Ruth?"

"Yes. I want this stopped as much as you. I'll take care of it and give you a call."

"Thank you. Please keep this between you and your mother. I don't want the killer to know what we're doing."

"I want him caught, too." Josh started back toward the door into the house.

When they entered, Gabriel was in the kitchen, leaning against the counter with his arms and feet crossed. He pushed off and assessed her.

She smiled. "Josh will help us."

"Don't get the idea I'm helping you, Michaels. I'm helping the assistant DA and the police."

"Oh, don't worry. I've never had those illusions." Gabriel strode to the front door and held it open for Kira.

She turned to Josh. "Thanks, again. Hopefully this nightmare will be over soon." Then she left, feeling for the first time that they had a chance to find the killer.

As Larry drove in the direction of her house, Gabriel took her hand and wove his fingers through hers. "I know you feel this will give us the answer, but it might not. I do think we need to look into the other three women even more and see what they have in common. I would have said age until Mary Lou was killed. She's five years younger than Marcie. Rebecca and Shirley were months apart in age and only a year older than Marcie."

"I agree. They all have different hair and eye color. They were in good shape, a little on the thin side. Penny can help with that."

As Larry pulled into her driveway, Kira checked her watch. "She'll be here in five or ten minutes."

Inside, Larry went through the house to make sure no one was there, and then he took up his position in the living room. Penny arrived on time with a box of information and set it on the dining room table. Gabriel hooked up Kira's computer while Penny brought two laptops from the office.

"Chief Shaffer's going to be here soon," Penny said as she sat at one end.

While Kira took the place opposite her secretary, Gabriel folded his tired body into the chair between the ladies.

Penny pulled a couple of sheets out of the box. "I've started a list of characteristics and interests between the victims, but there's still more that needs to be done. Like places they frequented."

"Let's each take one of them and delve into their lives. I'll do Rebecca. Penny can have Shirley, and Gabriel, Mary Lou. We know Marcie the best, but we'll flesh out her profile after we finish with these ladies.

Going to Pinecrest High School and being in the youth group are two things they all have in common. What else?"

With a grimace, Gabriel opened his laptop and began typing.

Kira was investigating mutual friends when her cell phone rang. She saw it was her grandmother and hurried to answer the call. "Hi, Grams."

"Kira, I'm in pain and need your help."

NINE

Kira's cell phone began to slide from her hand. She caught it before it hit the table. "I've got to go to Grams' house. She's in trouble." Did the killer come after her grandmother? Kira shot to her feet, snatched her purse from the table, and rushed for the kitchen door.

Then she remembered Grams was on the phone. Kira put it up to her ear. "Grams, are you still there?"

Nothing.

Gabriel grasped her arm and stopped her from leaving through the garage. "Larry will drive us. Let's go out the front."

Us. Each day they'd worked together as

partners in this investigation had firmed their friendship. Kira changed directions. She didn't see any reason the killer would go after her grandmother. She needed to remain calm. Grams was eighty and didn't fit into the victim category for the murderer.

Positioned at the front door, Larry opened it when he saw Kira and Gabriel. "I heard. I'll put on the siren."

Kira's heart rate accelerated as the police cruiser did. "She said she was hurt. In trouble. Should I call an ambulance?"

Gabriel slipped his arm around her shoulders. "We're almost there."

Kira spied the house half a block away. A minute later with Gabriel and Larry beside her, she raced for the porch while fumbling to get her key out.

When she entered her grandmother's place, she called out. "Grams, where are you?"

"In the kitchen."

Kira hurried into the room, her breathing shallow, her chest aching. Grams lay on the floor by the refrigerator in the midst of glass shards. Blood flowed from several cuts. "What happened?"

"I thought I cleaned up all the water on the floor, but I didn't. I slipped, dropped my drink, and fell. I tried to get up but couldn't."

"You're bleeding a lot."

"I'm on blood thinner."

Kira looked at Larry. "Wouldn't it be faster if you take her to the hospital in your car?"

He nodded.

While Gabriel and the police officer helped her grandmother to her feet and supported her between them, Kira grabbed some towels. That was when she saw the shard of glass sticking out the back of her grandmother's left leg.

"Wait." Kira knelt and examined the wound. It wasn't bleeding as much as the others. She didn't want to pull it out and have more blood loss than there already was. "Okay. Let's get her to the hospital."

Within half an hour, the emergency room doctor had removed the piece from her grandmother's leg, treated it, and stitched it up. Kira stood next to Grams, holding her hand. Gabriel and Larry were outside in the hallway.

Craig Addison, their family doctor, entered the room. "Beth, I heard you were brought in. What happened?"

"She dropped a glass in the kitchen, slipped, and fell," Kira answered because the ER attendant had given her grandmother a mild sedative. "She has five cuts that needed stitches, and then they're going to take an X-ray of her ankle. She couldn't put any weight on it."

The ER doctor glanced at Craig. "I'm cleaning up the ones that don't need stitches and making sure there are no splinters of glass still embedded. I suspect she has a fractured ankle. A few of the cuts wouldn't stop bleeding, so I gave her something to help the clotting."

"May I talk with you, Kira, in the corridor?" Craig smiled at Grams then headed to the door and waited for Kira.

In the hallway, Craig drew her to the side away from Gabriel and Larry. "This is the third time in eight months she's fallen.

If she hadn't been able to call you, she could have lost a lot of blood. Have her stay with you until she's better, especially if her ankle is broken. I'll come by and check on her. Plus, I'm also going to have an X-ray taken of her hip to make sure she hasn't broken it. Even a hair line crack will cause her problems."

"I'll do whatever needs to be done, but Grams is determined to be independent. Remember she didn't call me after one of those falls. She had a friend take her to the hospital because I was in court, and she didn't want to disturb me."

"That's why I'm talking to you. I'll also go back in and make things clear to her."

Kira smiled. "Thank you. She'll listen to you before me. I'm so glad you took over for your father last year. How's he doing in Florida?"

"Enjoying the warm weather. That's why he retired and moved. He said his bones ached too much in the winter in Oklahoma. He'd have probably retired five years earlier if he had lived further north."

While Craig went into the ER room to

talk with Grams, Kira moved to Gabriel and Larry. "He's going to convince my grandmother to stay at my house. I'll feel much better if she does, especially with what's happening in Pinecrest. We'll probably be here a few more hours."

"Do you want me to call Penny and let her know what's going on?" Larry asked.

"Yes and tell her to keep on top of getting the evidence from StarPoint. But until then, she can work on the list of similarities between the victims."

"I'm going back to the house to work with her. Larry will stay with you."

"But how about—"

"I can take care of myself. Your house is only five blocks, and it isn't snowing anymore."

Kira looked at Gabriel. "I wish you'd stay."

He pulled Kira away from her guard and leaned toward her right ear. "I need to do something. I'm antsy. I keep thinking we're missing something. I'm stopping by the police station. It's only a block out of my way." Gabriel shrugged, his eyes glinting.

"Besides, who knows? Bill Shaffer might take pity on me and give me a ride."

"What are you really up to, Gabriel Michaels?"

"Okay. I want to see how long it'll be until I get my truck back. I'm hoping they've finished going over it and sent it to the Premier Garage."

"I'll see you at my house later?"

"Yes. I'm not leaving your protection up to one police officer. But I figure you're safe with Larry in the middle of the ER." Gabriel waved to the police officer and strode toward the exit.

Watching him walk away made her realize how much she'd come to depend on him. He had a stake in this investigation. His presence gave her solace that there might be an end to this nightmare soon.

* * *

Gabriel crossed the street and walked in the direction of the police station. The fresh cold air smelled good after being in the hospital. He was glad this time it had nothing to do with the serial killer. He kept racking his brain trying to think of anything that Marcie had said to him those last months. There was a time last November when she had been skittish and tense. Abbey had even told him she'd heard her mother crying a couple of times in her bedroom. Then things started to change in December. When he read the last journal they had reviewed from the evidence, he'd gotten the sense she was scared. Why hadn't she said anything to him or her family? What had she written in the missing pages of the one journal? She was the key to this.

Gabriel entered the police station and nearly ran into Chief Shaffer who was leaving.

The man scowled "Why are you here? To confess?"

"After being shot at and in the hospital last night, I don't have the time to listen to the same old thing. You know I'm not guilty. When are you going to admit you messed up? Three more women are dead because you didn't do your job right in the first place."

Bill closed the space between them and stabbed his finger into Gabriel's chest. "Be careful with your accusations. I'm not someone you want as an enemy." His words were low and full of anger.

"What did I do to you? Or is it because you're on Ruth Morgan's payroll, too?"

The lines on his tanned face slashed deeper. "Marcie was too good for you. I used to hear stories from my dad about your reckless behavior in high school. You kept him busy as the police chief. Remember the time you raced Carson, and he ended up wrecking his car? He couldn't play football after that. He was the best receiver on our team. He wouldn't have done it if you hadn't goaded him."

The year Carson was a senior and Gabriel a sophomore, they had raced on the highway along with several others. There was a group of teenage boys who loved cars and loved to race. They usually did every weekend until that accident with Carson. "Yes, I was one of the guys racing Carson, not the only one. I won, but I didn't goad Carson. He was part of the group, actually the leader. We were just doing what we loved to do. Was it smart? No, but back then we all thought we were invincible. Haven't you done things you regret?"

Bill harrumphed. "Why are you here?"

"I wanted to see when my truck would be released to Premier Garage, and if you found any evidence pointing to who shot it."

"Your truck's at the garage. Other than the similarity in the bullets in Kira's car and your truck, no. I was heading out to talk to Evan Jones. His truck was seen on the traffic cam, leaving town not long before the incident. Also Al Nelson's and Pastor Dunkin's vehicles. With snow being predicted and the late hour, the road to the highway wasn't busy. Otherwise, nothing but the boot print, but I'm sure you already know that since you and Kira are working on this case. As I told her, don't interfere in my investigation. I won't hesitate to throw you in jail if you do."

Gabriel waited until the police chief left

then made his way to Al's Diner on Main Street between the station and the garage. He wasn't interfering. He would grab a cup of coffee he desperately needed and see what Al had been doing last night.

His cell phone rang a few steps away from the diner. "Is something wrong?" he asked Kira.

"Grams' ankle is broken, but they have to wait until the swelling goes down before they can cast her foot. I thought we'd be here for hours, but Craig has helped to move everything along faster. We'll be leaving soon. Are you at the house yet?"

"No. Bill released my truck. It's at the garage. I'm heading there to see when it'll be fixed. Jeremy might hurry it along."

"We can pick you up if you want."

"I'm fine. Quit worrying. I'll be at your house within the hour. Has your grandmother been giving you grief about having to stay with you?"

"No. I think she's relieved. See you soon."

Gabriel entered the diner and sat on a stool, not far from where Al stood. When not in the kitchen, he often served the people at the counter. When the owner came his way, Gabriel said, "I'd like some coffee to go."

Al set a cup in front of Gabriel and filled it nearly to the top. "You look like you need the caffeine. I heard this morning about what happened to you and Kira. Business has been slow ever since Mary Lou was found, but I can't blame people."

"Are you still staying open until ten?"

"Yes, but I don't leave until later, except for last night."

Al's house wasn't along the road where his car was captured on the traffic cam. "So you were home before it started to snow?"

"Not exactly. I gave Melinda a ride to her place. I've been doing that since Mary Lou went missing. Her husband drops her off on his way to work, but he doesn't get off until midnight."

Gabriel blew on the coffee then took a sip. "This is good as always. I'd better get moving. I need to check on my truck. I can't go long without it. I'm just glad the snow didn't stick or stay around for long."

The short walk to the garage only took five minutes. It sounded like Al had an alibi, but Gabriel would let the police follow up with Melinda. With Kira involved, he knew Bill would check all the leads. If it had just been him in the truck, he had his doubts. But then he remembered Bill's dad, the police chief in Pinecrest for twenty-five years. Bill was downright pleasant compared to his father.

When no one was out front, although a few cars were parked at the side of the building, Gabriel called out for Jeremy, the owner, and rang the bell that signaled a customer had arrived. Nothing. He had one other mechanic working for him part-time but only in the afternoon. This didn't feel right. Gabriel tossed his coffee cup in the trash, skirted the counter, and headed for the door that led to the work area.

When he stepped into the large garage, not one sound filled the air. Gabriel spied his truck in the second bay. As he approached, all his senses sharpened. If Jeremy had left he would have locked up when his part-time helper wasn't there.

Besides, Jeremy's car was parked at the side. Who owned the other vehicle?

"Jeremy," he called out several more times as he walked around his truck.

On the other side, he found a set of legs covered with Jeremy's blue uniform and black boots sticking out from under the vehicle. Gabriel knelt and leaned down to look under the truck.

"Jeremy, are you okay?"

Still no response.

He thought of pulling Jeremy out by the feet, but if he was hurt, he didn't want to harm him anymore by moving him the wrong way. Instead, Gabriel removed his overcoat, got his flashlight out of his glove compartment, and then wiggled under his truck. Alongside Jeremy, he could see the mechanic's eyes were closed. As Gabriel checked Jeremy's neck for a pulse, his fingers encountered a wet substance. Gabriel shone the light on his hand, red with blood.

TEN

Kira shut the drapes in the spare bedroom then turned to see if her grandmother needed anything before she left her alone to rest, but Grams' eyes were already shut, and her chest rose and fell gently. Kira tiptoed into the hallway and quietly closed the door.

When she entered the living room, she looked around. "Gabriel isn't back yet?"

Larry shook his head as he opened the front door to do a walk around the house.

"You've got it bad for that man," Penny said from the dining room.

Heat singed Kira's cheeks. "He was shot last night. I think I have a reason to be concerned about him."

Her secretary jotted something on a piece of paper then glanced at her. "Yep, I know that look. There's more than concern in it."

"Yes, embarrassment."

"I'm sure he'll be here soon. Maybe Jeremy and he began talking about cars or trucks. You know how men can get when they do."

"Any progress on the women's profiles?"

"Nothing that they all have in common. They go to different hairdressers, grocery stores, and so on."

"I'll call Gabriel then help you."

Penny's cell phone rang, blaring one of the latest country western songs. "Hello." Her secretary listened to the other person on the line, slowly the corner of her mouth turning down. "Okay, I'll let Kira know. Someone will come pick up a copy of the report." When Penny disconnected, she said, "We got the information from StarPoint, but they only keep the past twelve months. All we'll get is the last five weeks of Marcie's life."

"Let's hope that's enough. Larry and I will pick it up at the police station if you'll peek in and make sure Grams is doing okay a couple of times. She's sleeping and probably will for a while."

"I will. Are you swinging by the garage to see if Gabriel's there?"

"You know me too well."

Kira sat in the front of the patrol car with Larry. The first stop was the police station because it was closer. When she went inside, she'd hoped that Bill was there.

After getting a copy of the StarPoint data, Kira asked the dispatcher/ receptionist, "Where's Bill?"

"He's talking to the people on the traffic cam who were driving on the highway where the shooting was last night."

"Like who?"

"Al at the diner, Pastor Dunkin, and the elementary school principal."

"Will you have the chief call when he returns?" She wanted to know how the interviews went. She couldn't see any of those men being the shooter.

"It'll probably be within the hour. Oh, I forgot. I have a copy of Mary Lou's autopsy for you. It just came in, too. I put the other one on the police chief's desk."

Kira walked back and took the report in a manila envelope then started to leave but paused. "Did Gabriel Michaels come in here?"

"Yes about half an hour ago. He was going to the garage."

After returning to the patrol vehicle, Kira laid back against the headrest. "Gabriel's probably gone from the garage, but let's check. I didn't see him on the street walking to my house."

When Larry pulled up at the Premier Garage, Kira quickly exited the car. She looked down Fourth Avenue and didn't see him heading toward her place. Her steps quickened the closer she was to the building. Was Jeremy almost through with his truck, so Gabriel was waiting?

As she entered the front area of the garage, it was empty. She frowned. "Must be in the back."

"I'll go first." Larry came around the counter and strode to the rear door. He opened it, his body blocking Kira's view. "Gabriel. Jeremy."

The quiet taunted Kira. She pushed past the patrol officer and called out, "Gabriel."

Still nothing.

As she moved further into the three-bay garage, the silence ate at her composure. The building was wide open.

Her heartbeat hammered against her skull, echoing through her head. Her stomach knotted. "Okay, Gabriel isn't here, but where is Jeremy? His car's at the side of the garage."

Larry slid his gun out of the holster and pointed it toward the concrete floor. "I don't like this. Stay behind me."

A moan penetrated the stillness.

Kira tensed.

Larry lifted his gun and held it out in front of him.

When they skirted the front of Gabriel's truck, another groan floated on the air. Her gaze riveted to legs sticking out from under the F-150. They moved, and she gasped.

She hurried forward. From the pants that were showing, she could tell it wasn't Gabriel, so it had to be Jeremy.

She glanced under the vehicle. "It's Jeremy." She lifted her head and peered over her shoulder at Larry who was panning the garage. "He's hurt, I think. There's a flashlight under there but shining away from Jeremy."

Larry knelt next to her and checked out the situation. "I'm calling this in. I saw evidence of a struggle in front of Gabriel's truck."

While Larry rose and withdrew his phone, Kira scooched under the truck to Jeremy, the light glaring in her eyes, making it hard to tell exactly what occurred.

He rolled his head toward her, opening his dazed eyes. "Kira...?"

"What happened?" That was when Kira positioned the pink flashlight on Jeremy and saw the blood on the concrete floor. Then she recalled Gabriel asking her to hand her a flashlight similar to that one when he'd exited his truck the night she'd been shot at and she'd needed her purse. She'd dug it out of his glove compartment. If this was the same one, how had it gotten here?

Jeremy's eyes slid shut for a moment. "I don't know—how—I got—here. My head hurts. Did I—fall?"

Her mind raced with various scenarios, but they all came back to one question: how did Gabriel's flashlight get under the truck. "I don't think so. Do you remember seeing Gabriel this morning?"

"No."

"Was someone else in the garage this morning besides you?"

"Craig Addison."

"When?"

"First thing—worked on his car. Mayor, too." Jeremy began inching out. He grimaced, sucked in a breath, and stopped.

"Stay put until the paramedics come."

"Head spinning."

Larry ducked down. "The paramedics have arrived. So has the police chief."

"Help is here, Jeremy. I'm going to give them room to work on you." Kira wiggled her way out from under the truck. Then one paramedic took her place while the second one went around to the other side.

Larry helped Kira to her feet. "Chief Shaffer wants to talk to you." He nodded toward Bill at the front of the F-150.

Kira joined him, her gaze drawn to fresh blood on the concrete and bumper. "Do you think that's Jeremy's blood?"

"Probably. Someone must have hit him with this lug wrench then hid him under the truck."

"Why?"

"Don't know. Hopefully Jeremy will be able to tell us."

"He doesn't remember what happened to him."

"He might in time."

Kira thought about the pink flashlight. "Just a minute. I need to check on something." She headed to Gabriel's glove compartment and opened it. The only things inside were maps. She returned to Bill. "This may be connected to the case. Gabriel and I wondered how the shooter knew we were going to be on the highway.

Maybe something like a GPS tracker had been put on the truck."

"You think the killer did this so he could remove the tracker?"

"It's possible. The pink flashlight under the truck was in Gabriel's glove compartment."

"He was looking under the truck?"

She prayed Gabriel left before the attack on Jeremy. "I don't know. I'm calling Gabriel. He was coming here. That might narrow down the time the killer attacked Jeremy or whoever did this." She hoped so because the alternative might be that something happened to Gabriel—something far worse than what happened to Jeremy. As she removed her cell phone from her pocket, her gaze latched onto the blood on the floor. What if it wasn't Jeremy's but Gabriel's?

Kira hit *call* on her phone and a ringtone like Gabriel's sounded in the garage. She locked gazes with Bill. "His phone is here." She strode toward the truck's driver's side where the ringing sounded.

"Let me look." Bill stepped in front of her, put gloves on, and searched under the seat. Gingerly he extracted the cell phone.

* * *

A groan pierced through the throbbing pain pulsating in Gabriel's skull. He inched his eyes open partway. Darkness enveloped him. His cheek rested against a frigid slab, the cold shivering through him. He tried to move. His hands and feet were tied together. Rope dug into his wrists.

He closed his eyes for a moment, trying to figure out what happened. Vague images flitted across his foggy mind. In the garage. Under his truck. Blood on his hand. But how did he get here? Where was he?

The increasingly rapid beat of his heart lured him back toward the void.

* * *

When Larry finally drove Kira home, Penny opened the front door before Kira had a chance to insert her key.

"Anything new?" Penny glanced between Kira and Larry.

"No. Gabriel hasn't called, has he?"

Her secretary shook her head.

"Is Grams up yet?" Kira walked toward the hallway.

"No. I've been peeking in every ten minutes or so. What should we do?"

The doorbell rang. Kira halted and swung around while Larry checked before letting in the police chief.

Kira came back into the foyer. "We have to assume the person who attacked Jeremy has Gabriel since he's missing. We need to find him before he kills him." *The memory of Jeremy's nasty fracture on the back of his head mocked her statement. Gabriel can't be dead. Please, Lord. I can't lose him.*

Bill gestured toward the papers in Kira's hand. "I agree. Let's look over the information from StarPoint and see if there's a location Marcie visited that might help us connect the dots."

She handed the paperwork to the police chief. "I need to see how Grams is doing.

I'll be right back." Kira quickly looked in on her grandmother, sleeping peacefully.

Back in the dining room, Bill gave each person a copy of the report. Kira had asked the receptionist at the police station to make three copies and now she was glad she had. Patterns would be easier to see if they went through the whole five weeks.

"Mark anything that's repeated. Then we'll list those places." Bill took the chair where Gabriel had been earlier. "I'm gonna look over Mary Lou's autopsy."

Every time she glanced at the police chief, Kira's chest constricted and her breathing became shallow. *When did my feelings for Gabriel change?*

* * *

Gabriel struggled to loosen the rope around his wrists. It was only a matter of time before his captor returned and killed him. But worse he might go after Kira. He couldn't let that happen.

What if he was at the garage? Jeremy's part-time mechanic should be arriving soon. That ray of hope spurred him on.

Wincing, Gabriel rolled over onto his back, trapping his hands beneath him. Then he rocked until he could sit up, his effort aggravating his gunshot wound. He pushed away thoughts of his pain as much as possible. He needed to know where he was. Maybe there was something that could help him get loose. He wouldn't give up and wait for the murderer to kill him. He had people depending on him—Abbey, Jessie—Kira.

He scooched forward like an earthworm. Where was he? The floor beneath him felt like a garage? Or maybe it was a basement? Or a warehouse?

When his feet hit a solid wall, he contemplated which way to go. He went right, pressing his side against it. Unless the place was empty, he should run into something. The pain continued to drill into his head, but he couldn't let it slow him down. He kept focused on his task to free himself. When he encountered another wall, he inched around to follow its length.

With no idea how long he'd been here,

a sense of urgency plagued him. If the murderer brought him here and left, he had something planned. Or why wouldn't he have already killed him?

Kira.

The psychopath was going after her. She would be his fifth victim—unless he could escape and get to her in time. An image of her filled his mind, prodding him to move faster.

He ran into a barrier. A cot? He maneuvered around it, stopping partway down it. Using the bed, he managed to get to his knees without falling over. He folded his body over the edge of the piece of furniture, the side of his face smashed into the smelly mattress. As he struggled to his feet, he inched further onto the bed. One odor overrode all others—blood.

He wanted to recoil, but he couldn't stop. If he could stand, he might be able to find a light switch and something to cut the ropes.

Was this where he killed the women before disposing of their bodies? The thought churned his stomach, but it also urged him to move even faster.

When he stood upright finally, he continued his exploration along the wall and prayed he'd find a light switch before he was discovered.

Lord, I can't do this without You. I need to get to Kira.

* * *

Kira looked up. "What do you mean they couldn't tell if the bullet in Mary Lou came from the same gun as the others?"

Bill frowned. "Exactly that. It wasn't in her body. They had nothing to compare it to."

"But she was shot like the others?"

"Yes, as well as cut up. A paper was stuffed in her mouth, too."

Time was running out. Kira firmed her resolve to end this now. "I found another location Marcie went to ten times in five weeks. Near Pinecrest Lake."

Penny added it to the list of places Marcie continuously visited. "What could that be?"

Bill put a pin into a map of the area he'd mounted on the dining room wall. "Probably a cabin, although there is a marina not too far from there. That looks the most promising. Isolated. Surrounded by woods."

"Any more?" Penny asked.

"Besides the Morgan Estate, a few stores, Abbey's school, and Gabriel's ranch, that's the only other place frequented much. I'm going to go out there with two officers." Bill grabbed his sheepskin overcoat and cowboy hat. "I've got to do something."

The police chief voiced how Kira felt. "What if you don't find anything?"

"Then I'll visit the places she went to less."

"How about the Morgan Estate?" Kira asked, preparing for an eruption of outrage.

"What are you implying?" Bill hovered near Kira, his large bulky body blocking her from rising.

"Their estate is large and a lot of people work for them. What if Marcie was seeing someone employed by the Morgans?" Kira could see her friend doing that because Marcie was constantly doing things her mother would disapprove of.

His narrowed eyes bore into her. "If I do that, then I need to check Gabriel's ranch, too. She went there a lot."

"Because Abbey stays there a lot, but go ahead. We've ruled out Gabriel. That only leaves Hank living there." Kira had never thought of Hank as a possibility, but he could be. He certainly was nearby when she was shot at, and he knew about their plans to go to Oklahoma City.

"So you think it's Hank?" Penny asked, getting to her feet with her mug.

"No, but this guy has gone almost a year undetected, so we probably need to think outside the box."

Bill headed toward the foyer. "Larry, keep these two safe. Penny, see if you can locate who owns that property at the lake. I'll call y'all with what I find."

Larry locked the door.

Penny walked into the kitchen and returned with the pot of coffee. "I noticed your mug was near empty."

"Thanks. I need something to keep me going." Kira rose. "I'm checking on Grams. She should have been up by now."

* * *

When Gabriel's left shoulder encountered a bump that felt like a light switch, he used his arm to flip it on. A faint glow illuminated the center of what must be a large basement room. Along the walls, dim shadows lurked. His gaze swept over the mattress. The sight of the blood stains nauseated him. He quickly looked away.

The only other furniture in the cavernous space was a worktable with tools on it across from him. He shoved aside his thoughts about what those tools could have been used for and started across.

Inch by inch, he made his way to the other side of the room. The only thing he thought could work would be the big saw. Minutes ticked away, his progress slow. He kept his mind focused on the tool and on saving Kira.

Once she'd realized her mistake in prosecuting him last spring, she'd thrown herself totally into finding the actual murderer. And if he was honest, that would be the only way all the townspeople would believe he was innocent. He'd never cared what others thought of him, but he had a daughter to consider. This was her home.

When he reached the table, he slowly rotated until his back was against the wooden ledge. He leaned backwards with his elbows cocked, his fingers creeping closer and closer.

His thumb and forefinger grabbed a corner of the saw, and then he slowly drew it toward him. Finally he could grasp the sharp teeth of the tool. The blade sliced into his hand as he maneuvered it around. At the edge of the table, he tried to clasp the saw more securely.

The blade's teeth dug into his palm. He dropped his grip, and the saw crashed to the floor. A loud noise echoed through the room.

ELEVEN

Kira paced the dining room, going over and over the other places Marcie had gone to during that five-week window. Nothing jumped out at her—except the elementary school.

"I know who the lake property belongs to." Penny pumped her arm into the air. "Evan Jones. He inherited it from his aunt and uncle a couple of years ago."

Kira halted behind Penny and looked over her shoulder at the computer screen. "That explains why she went to the school so much. I never had the sense Abbey was having difficulties in her class, and Marcie didn't volunteer. She'd always preferred to throw money at a problem rather than do something personally. Maybe she was paying Evan a visit."

"But too many stops would have raised gossip, and I would have heard about that. I know the principal's secretary. I'll give her a call."

"Wait until we hear from Bill. We don't want to tip Evan that we're on to him if he's the killer."

"I don't know about being the murderer, but he's good looking and has always captured women's interest. I feel sorry for his wife. Liz almost left him once right before you returned to town."

"Is there anything you don't know?" Kira checked her watch. Bill should be at the cabin by now. The waiting was driving her crazy.

"Who the killer is. I wish I did. It would have saved a lot of heartache."

When Kira's cell phone rang, she rushed to the other end of the table to grab it. "What did you find?" she asked when she noted it was Bill.

"A cabin that looks deserted. I have an

officer trying to get a warrant although our evidence is flimsy. Who owns it?"

"The elementary school principal, Evan Jones." The doorbell sounded, and Larry immediately went into the foyer.

"Really? If I can't get a warrant, I'll go pick the man up and question him."

"That'll get tongues wagging in Pinecrest." Kira shifted until she had a view of the entry hall and who was at the door.

"I'll give him an opportunity to tell me why Marcie visited him and see if he'll give me permission to search his cabin. Hang tight. I've got a feeling we're close."

When Larry opened the door, he blocked Craig from coming inside. "Just a second, Bill." Kira cupped her hand over the microphone and said to the officer guarding her, "I asked him to come check on Grams." She smiled at the doctor as he entered then said into the phone, "Evan's car was one of the vehicles on the traffic cam."

"Yes, but his wife vouched for him. He was at home. If she was lying to me, she might change her mind."

"Keep me posted. I'll let Larry know."

"He needs to stay there until we have the killer in custody."

"He will. I'll have Penny go get us something to eat." Kira tapped the off button, pocketed her phone, and strolled toward Craig. "I'm glad you could come. Grams has been sleeping all afternoon. Her pulse rate is normal, and she doesn't have a fever, but I thought she would be up by now. I just want to make sure she's all right."

"Of course, I'll check her. Her body went through a trauma. Rest is a normal reaction to that."

"Not usually for Grams." Kira showed him the way to the spare bedroom her grandmother was staying in. She pushed the door open and turned on the overhead light. "See...that usually would wake her. Earlier I talked to her for a few minutes, went to get her a cup of hot tea, and when I came back, she was asleep again."

"Exhaustion will do that to you." He removed his stethoscope from his black bag.

"Penny is going to get some food for us. Would you like to join us?" She'd rather have people around her until Bill let her know about the cabin. She needed to keep her mind off what could have happened to Gabriel. She had to leave it in the Lord's hands.

"I wish I could, but I have another place I need to be."

Kira left Craig alone with Grams to talk to Penny about getting hamburgers and fries while they waited for Bill to call or come by. She wanted to go to the police station and be there when they brought Evan in for questioning, but she didn't want to leave Grams alone any more than she already had.

Please let this be over soon, God. Gabriel doesn't deserve this.

* * *

Sitting on the floor with the saw propped against the leg of the worktable, Gabriel sliced the rope until he could wiggle and twist out of his bonds. His arms, especially

239

his injured one, protested. When he brought them around and looked at his hands, blood coated them from the cuts of the blade's teeth.

After freeing his bound ankles, he mounted the steps to the door. He tried the handle. Locked. As he descended the stairs, he paused and clutched the railing. His vision swirled in the dim light. He sat and closed his eyes. His head throbbed. The seconds became a minute then another.

God was with him. He could do this. Using the railing, he pulled himself up and continued down the stairs. At the worktable, he snatched the sledgehammer, climbed the steps again, and smashed the lock and door with the tool.

The damaged piece of wood flew open after five swings of the tool. He moved out into the hallway and tried to get his bearings. Where was he? He went to the left and found the kitchen. While he looked for any indication of whose home he was in, he wrapped a dishtowel around the hand bleeding the worst.

He searched for a phone as he moved

through the first floor. Like so many people in today's times, he couldn't find a landline. Before he left the living room, a photo on an end table caught his attention. Craig Addison in a cap and gown holding a diploma.

Stunned, he stared at his family doctor.

Bile rose in his throat. He gritted his teeth and charged for the front door.

He was also Kira's family doctor. He needed to warn Kira. With Grams accident, the doctor could use a visit to Kira's house to do the unthinkable. Exhausted, he forced every ounce of strength into his legs. The doctor lived on several acres right outside Pinecrest. Gabriel began loping toward town, looking for the nearest phone. Each breath he dragged into his lungs burned, but he wouldn't stop until he reached Kira.

* * *

After Penny left Kira's house to pick up some dinner, Larry locked the door. Kira eased into a lounge chair, tempted to raise the footrest and recline back. But if she did, she would fall asleep. She laid her cell phone on a nearby table. She didn't want to rest until Bill called to tell her Evan was the killer, Gabriel was found safe, and Grams was all right.

"So Chief Shaffer might have a lead on the murderer?" Larry asked as he fitted his tall, lanky body onto the couch across from Kira.

"Hopefully, and we'll find out where Gabriel is. I'm sure the killer took him. Bill is going to keep me informed."

She couldn't sit any longer no matter how much she wanted to. Craig hadn't left yet. She needed to see what he said about her grandmother. She shoved to her feet. "I'll be with Grams."

"How is she doing?" the police officer asked.

"Resting more than she usually does, but then she has been through a trauma. I'm just used to her being so active she could put me to shame."

A few seconds later, Kira appeared in the entrance to the spare bedroom. Her grandmother sat in bed with several pillows propping her up.

Grams glanced at her and smiled. "Can't a gal get some sleep without everyone worrying?"

"Sure, just as soon as you let me know that's what you're doing. You hardly ever rest." Kira sat on the bed and took Grams' hand that wasn't bandaged. "How's your ankle doing?"

"It hurts like the dickens, but I can bare this. I'll let you sign my cast when I get it." Her grandmother winked at Kira then shifted her attention to Craig. "And Craig, you can sign my cast, too." Grams looked back at Kira. "I should be able to get one in the next day or so according to my doctor. Then I'll be following you around, Kira."

She laughed. "I'd like that, Grams, but only if the doctor says you can."

"I'd like her to rest until then. The swelling in her ankle is starting to go down. She lost some blood which makes her feel weak, but she'll be as good as new in no time."

"Thanks for coming." Kira rose to walk with Craig into the hallway to make sure there wasn't anything else he needed to tell her that he didn't want her grandmother to hear. "I'll be back in a minute, Grams."

"Take your time. If my eyes are closed, I'm just resting them."

"Okay," Kira said with a chuckle, but all humor fled her the second she was alone with Craig. "Will she really be all right?"

"Yes. I did get the results back on a couple of the blood tests I ran in the hospital. Her iron level is down which is adding to her tiredness, but rest and some medication I'm going to prescribe will help with that. I'll call it in to the pharmacy. I gave her something for the pain even though she said she could bare it. And thankfully her hip isn't fractured. This time next week she'll be back to her old self."

Kira took Craig's hand. "Thank you. I'm so glad you took over for your dad. Grams has been going to an Addison most of her life. She hates changes."

"How about you?"

"I'm an assistant DA. I've learned to go with the changes. I've had my share of surprises, especially lately. Larry will let you out." She squeezed his hand gently then released it and walked back into her grandmother's room.

She needed to spend some time with Grams while she was awake. Until she heard from Bill, there was little she could do other than pray. She hoped Evan would tell them where Gabriel was. She didn't want to think about what would happen if he were dead.

* * *

Gabriel left the Henderson's porch. Even though their lights blazed in the darkness creeping over the land, no one answered his knocks. He headed down the long driveway back to the road. Pinecrest was probably no more than a mile, but at the moment that seemed like a hundred while he put one foot in front of the other.

As he left the Henderson's place, headlights came toward him from town. Gabriel started to flag the car down, but something stopped him. Craig could be returning to his house. He couldn't risk it.

He had a better chance getting to town on his own or finding someone home to help him.

Gabriel ducked behind a bush near the side of the road. As the car sped past him, he noted the luxury car, the same one parked at the side of Jeremy's garage. It was too dark to get a good look at the driver, but it was probably Craig. He would have to assume that and travel toward town away from the road. When Craig discovered he was gone, the doctor would come after him. He knew his secret.

Too exhausted to jog anymore, Gabriel trudged through the thick dense vegetation about a hundred feet from the road. In the dark, he stumbled a couple of times, but he caught himself and kept going. All he had to do was get to town, find a phone, call the police to let them know about Craig, then make sure Kira was all right. He needed to see her with his own eyes. The thought of something happening to her kept him trudging through the underbrush.

He glimpsed some lights in the woods. The sight of them spurred him faster. Until his foot came down in a hole, and he tumbled forward.

* * *

"Grams, are you sure you don't want any of this soup from Al's Diner?" Kira asked as she sat next to her grandmother's bed.

"Hon, I'm tired. That roll from Al's is all I want. He should open a bakery. Delicious." Grams yawned. "I don't need you to sit in here and watch me sleep." Her grandmother snuggled under the covers. "Turn the light off on your way out and shut the door."

Kira kissed her on the cheek then left the bedroom. When she entered the living room, she found Wally there. He had replaced Larry half an hour ago. "Where's Penny?"

"She went home, but she wanted you to call her whatever time of the day you find the killer."

"Have you heard anything from Chief Shaffer?"

"He's at the cabin with Evan Jones the

last I heard."

She wanted to be there, too. She wanted to interrogate the principal. She was going crazy holed up in her house. Waiting.

Where is Gabriel? Is he alive?

As tired as she was, she couldn't sleep. She prowled the living room. "Why isn't the police chief calling? Surely he knows something by now."

No reply from Wally. He didn't talk like Larry. Right now she wished the young officer was here keeping her company.

When her cell phone rang, she grabbed it off the table she'd placed it on. "Any news, Bill?"

"Not what you want to hear."

His first words deflated her hope, and she sank onto the lounge chair. "What did you find at the cabin?"

"Evidence of a lover's tryst with some of the toys Evan liked to use. Maybe the wrong word is lover because what Marcie and Evan did here wasn't what I call love. Domination maybe. Sadistic definitely."

"So Marcie's lover was Evan."

"Yes, according to him for several years. At first he would meet her in Oklahoma City away from Pinecrest. Then when he inherited the cabin, they met there."

"So he's our killer? Can he tell us where Gabriel is?"

"No and no."

She nearly crushed her cell phone in her grip. "He's lying. The evidence points to him."

"For now, he has an ironclad alibi for Shirley's disappearance. He was at a national workshop in Chicago as one of the speakers, and when Marcie went missing, he and his wife were on a long weekend in Denver where her family lives. I'm in the process of verifying each time he was gone. According to Evan, his wife is aware of his—taste and has looked the other way when he indulges in them. He did say one interesting tidbit. Marcie was seeing someone else and not meeting with him much those last six weeks."

"Did he know who?" Her shoulders slumped forward, and she rested her elbows on her thighs.

"No."

"He wasn't jealous or upset about it?"

"He already had another woman satisfying his weird peccadillo. Rebecca."

"Not Shirley or Mary Lou?" Kira's eyes burned with fatigue. This wasn't over.

"No. I'm keeping him at the station until I get all the evidence to clear him."

"So there was no sign of Gabriel at the cabin?" She had pinned her hopes on Gabriel being there and alive.

"No, but I have my officers looking for him, and the sheriff's deputies are, too."

It wasn't enough. She wanted to be out there scouring the town for him. She was so afraid that he would end up like the women—dead, his body disposed of somewhere to be found later. The very thought sent her hope spiraling downward.

"I want to keep a police officer guarding you. The killer is linked to you somehow."

"Thanks. Call me if you hear anything about Gabriel."

"I will. Sorry. I wanted this to be the answer to what's going on here."

"So did I." Kira disconnected, set her phone on the table, leaned back in the lounge chair, closing her eyes. "It's not the principal so we're back to square one."

"Ma'am, I suggest you get some rest like your grandmother. You can't do much when you're this tired."

What Wally said made sense. She didn't think she could sleep, but maybe at least she would close her eyes and rest on her bed. She needed to if she was going to find the killer. The lead she thought would give her the identity of the murderer didn't pan out. There was another man Marcie became involved with. But who was he?

Slowly Kira trudged toward her bedroom, collapsed on her bed, and stretched out to rest for a while before digging into what evidence they had. Gabriel was out there somewhere, and she had to find him. She never wanted to tell Abbey her father was dead, too.

Tears stung her eyes. Kira shut them and tried to concentrate on calming thoughts...

A ringing sound penetrated her

exhausted mind. She rolled over, her gaze focusing on the red digital numbers on her clock. Ten after eight at night. She must have slept. She fumbled for her cell phone on the bedside table. Nothing. Did she leave it in the living room? Maybe. She'd been so tired she could have.

She pushed up then swung her legs off the bed and stood. She teetered for a second. Slowly her foggy brain cleared, and she still heard the phone ringing, but this time two different ringtones. Moving faster, she made her way down the hall to the living room. As she crossed to her cell on the table by the lounge chair, she wondered where Wally was. The other ringing was coming from the kitchen.

She picked the phone up, and it stopped. Probably went to voice mail. She started for the kitchen to find Wally, when that one ceased, too. She entered the room while her ringtone sliced through the silence again.

As she noticed it was Bill calling, her look fixed on Wally lying on the floor, his throat slit. Before she could do anything, strong arms locked across her chest and pressed her against a tall body.

TWELVE

Gabriel hoisted himself through an unlocked window on the side of Kira's house. It should have been locked. The very sight of it being open when he arrived honed his determination to save Kira. He'd called the police, and they were on the way, but was he too late? The sound of the sirens coming from different directions indicated they were a few minutes away, but a lot could happen in that amount of time.

In the room, he glimpsed Grams sleeping on the bed. The dim light from the neighbor's security lamp and her steady breathing showed him that she was unharmed. He hurried into the hallway, listening for any noise.

The quiet unnerved him.

* * *

Kira's self-defense training kicked in. She slammed her right boot into her attacker's knee then scraped it down the man's lower leg and stomped on his foot. His hold loosened enough that she dropped down while she lifted her arms up breaking the hold. She swung around and kicked his groin, her gaze intent on his body, not his face.

Craig stepped back, clasping himself for a few seconds while swear words spewed from him. Shock rooted her to the floor. She'd let him into her house, left him alone with Grams. What did he do to allow him accessed to her house?

The sound of sirens nearing fueled her surge of adrenaline. Craig blocked one of two exits from the kitchen. She spun toward the other one and ran for the door that led outside. As she grabbed for the knob, Craig charged her.

She concentrated on getting outside and around front. She needed to save Grams. She slammed the door open and rushed out of the kitchen.

A cry of rage shuddered down her length. Craig was gone from the doorway. She couldn't stop to see what was happening. She pumped her legs as fast as she could go. Her steps pounded against the ground and her heart against her rib cage.

She reached the front yard as several police officers poured out of their vehicles and raced toward her. She pointed toward the house. "The killer—Craig Addison—is inside—kitchen."

Two officers went around the back while more arrived and split off with half approaching the porch.

* * *

Gabriel leaped on Craig and dragged him down to the kitchen floor, rolling over and pinning the killer. He lifted a fist and hammered it into the doctor's face. Over and over.

When someone put a hand on his shoulder, he shook it away, determined Craig wouldn't escape.

"The police are here," Kira's voice came from the backdoor.

The words registered along with the fact that Craig was unconscious, and the kitchen was full of officers with their guns out and trained on them.

Gabriel threw his arms up in the air and rose.

Several police swarmed in on Craig. One officer felt for a pulse and rolled him over to handcuff him.

Gabriel focused on the one nearest him. Bill.

The police chief nodded at him. "Good job."

Gabriel glanced down at his clothes, covered in blood—some his own. If they hadn't arrived, he might have killed Craig. Cold anger had driven him until he'd trapped Craig. Then rage as he never experienced took over.

A hand clasped his arm. He looked to the side to see Kira, worry deep in her eyes.

"I'm okay. How about you?" He turned toward her, wanting to pull her into his arms and kiss her. But he didn't.

* * *

In the past thirty-six hours, Kira had gone from one emotion to another—fear, fury, relief, worry, shock, and grief at another death. Now the overriding feeling consuming her was worry. After Gabriel was seen at the hospital and released, he gave Bill his statement of events from the time he went to the garage to check on his truck. Then he walked out of the police station and disappeared.

She received a call twelve hours ago from Jessie letting her know that Gabriel was in Florida and bringing Abbey and her home soon. Kira had wanted to talk to him, but his sister had said he was holed up with Ruth Morgan in the library for the past few hours. Kira had hoped he would call when the meeting with Abbey's grandmother was through, but she couldn't imagine it lasting this long.

So now he didn't need her anymore. He was retrieving Abbey, who was the reason he helped her in the first place. She couldn't blame him for that.

But her heart cracked.

She cared—no—she loved him. She wanted more from him, but then she was the woman who fought so hard to put him in prison. At least the townspeople were safe now, and Craig was in jail.

Grams rolled her knee walker into her kitchen. "The coffee smells wonderful."

"Did you sleep all right?"

"Yes, how about you?" Her grandmother assessed her. "Never mind. I can tell you didn't. Gabriel will come back to Pinecrest."

"I know. This is his home."

"And I'm sure he'll come see you."

Kira wasn't sure about that. "What do you want me to fix you for breakfast?"

"The works. I haven't eaten in days. Then we need to get the Christmas decorations up, especially since you're going to stay with me for a few weeks."

"I'm not sure I ever want to go back to my house." The one time she went back to pack yesterday afternoon, her stomach roiled at the sight where Wally had been killed in her kitchen. The blood had been cleaned up, and all traces of a fight and his murder were gone, but she didn't want to live there. It would always remind her of Craig—and Gabriel.

"You can stay here as long as you need. So will you help me with decorating for Christmas? This year, more than ever before, Pinecrest has a lot to be thankful for. I do. Craig almost killed you—could have me."

"Gabriel stopped him from doing that. If he hadn't escaped from Craig's basement, managed to find a phone when he reached town, and let Bill know who the killer was, I might have died. The ringing of my phone and Wally's to warn us is what woke me." After Kira refilled her mug with coffee and poured one for Grams, she sat at the kitchen table.

"Maybe we'll have to do the decorating

in stages. I'm exhausted just from getting dressed and maneuvering in here. I have a feeling I'll be taking frequent breaks."

"You'll get no argument from me. I'm not in the Christmas mood." Kira gave Grams her mug.

"Maybe I can change your mind." Her grandmother took a sip while Kira settled in her chair. "I'm still in shock that the killer is Craig Addison. He's nothing like his father and grandfather. They were men of integrity. Why did he do it?"

"I'm not sure we'll ever know totally. When he was a kid, he was always so quiet and reserved. He didn't relate to others well. When he entered high school, he excelled in his schoolwork. He seemed to come out of his shyness a little. At his house they found a closet full of photos of Marcie from high school until right before he killed her. One of the photos was of her leaving Evan's lakeside cabin. The two were kissing. I think he snapped."

"But why the others?"

"I don't know. Rebecca used to go to the cabin, too, so that might have been the reason for her. But Mary Lou and Shirley didn't." Kira cupped her mug, relishing its warmth. For days, she'd been so cold deep in her bones.

The doorbell chimes resounded through the house.

"Are you expecting anyone, Grams?"

"No, unless it's the ladies from church. They're bringing some food by today. They think I'm an invalid."

When Kira checked out the peephole, she quickly opened the door to Bill. "Is something wrong?"

"Why does my presence mean there's something wrong?"

"Because you're the police chief. Come in." She stepped away to allow him inside.

Only coming in a few feet, Bill faced her. "I need you to come to the station. Craig Addison has agreed to confess to you only. If you don't come, he won't say a word."

"Does he have a lawyer?"

"Yes, and the lawyer approached me with this."

"He's going to confess to the murders?"

"I believe so."

"Let me tell Grams I'm leaving. Then I'll be down at the station."

Fifteen minutes later she sat catty-corner from Craig, who was shackled to the table. He dismissed his lawyer. When the man left, Craig turned to Kira and stared at her.

She wanted to flee and let the evidence alone convict him in court. She didn't want to be in a room alone with him even though she knew officers were on the other side of the glass, and this interview was being recorded. She was safe.

"I understand you want to tell me what you did and why." Suppressed emotions roughened her voice.

"I wanted you to stop me. Thank you for finally doing it."

"Why me?"

"You were always nice to me. In school, you noticed me. Others didn't."

"Is that why you killed Marcie and the other women?"

"Marcie betrayed me. Went out with me while she was seeing another man. She didn't deserve to live. Rebecca did the same thing. Cheated with Evan. She had to die."

"How about Shirley?"

"She was the worst one of them all. She used to make fun of me in high school. I decided to give her a chance to make up for that. Instead, she laughed in my face and said she could never go out with someone like me. That's when I knew she had to die, too."

The monotone of his voice chilled Kira. The marrow deep in her bones iced over.

* * *

Gabriel stood on the porch, gazing at his land. He and his family, as well as Ruth and Josh Morgan, had returned late last night. Abbey was still asleep, but he couldn't. Until he took care of some unfinished business, he wouldn't get any rest.

He had to see Kira today. When he'd nearly killed Craig in her kitchen, he hadn't realized that anger was still deep inside of him. The man had taken so much from him and his family, and Gabriel had been about to lose his humanity if he hadn't been stopped. That scared him to his core. He'd worked hard to live a life of integrity—still was striding for that. In a moment, he could have lost what he had.

Kira had shown him he could forgive a lot. His feelings for her were totally different from when they began working together. In a short time, he'd come to care deeply for her. No, that wasn't totally right. He was falling in love with her. She'd admitted what she'd done and wanted to make amends, and she had. Her life had been in danger the more she delved into the case, but that didn't stop her. She was going to show the whole town she had been wrong about him, and she did.

But he didn't want to pursue a relationship with her if he couldn't let go totally of his anger at what happened. That was why he had to see Ruth. Part of that fury was wrapped up in his relationship with his daughter's grandmother. If he could work something out with her for Abbey's sake, then maybe there was a chance to put his past behind him and move forward possibly with Kira in his life.

It had taken hours of negotiating and putting himself out there for Ruth to see, but she wasn't going to pursue custody of Abbey. His daughter would visit with her grandmother on a regular basis. He and Abbey were even going to Christmas Eve service with the Morgan family. It was a start.

Thank you, God. I see Your hand in this.

The sound of the front door opening reverberated through the cold air. He glanced over his shoulder. "I thought you were asleep."

Jessie smiled. "I've rested more in the past week than in months. I discovered I don't like the life of leisure."

"I appreciate you going with Abbey. I didn't have to worry about her with you there."

"Are you going to see her?"

"I have a feeling you're talking about Kira, not Ruth."

"Yes. You've changed."

He slanted a look at her. "How?"

"You're more grounded, accepting. Otherwise the long flight home would have been tension filled. You and Ruth were civil to each other."

"I'm learning hostility is tiring."

"So you're expecting me to be civil to the Morgans, too?"

"It would be nice, but that has to be your decision."

"I'll work on it. That's all I can promise. Go see Kira. I'm tired of you moping around."

He laughed. "I'm thinking, not moping. But I like your advice."

"I'm glad your truck was here when we returned. I might take Abbey into town later. We need to get a Christmas tree. We don't have much time to decorate it. This year we have a lot to be thankful for."

"Yes."

* * *

Kira left the interview room, emotionally ripped apart. To have Craig write and sign a confession would make the healing in town easier, but nothing would bring those women back. Once Craig had flipped out, he couldn't go back, and yet there was a part of him that had wanted to stop.

He'd always felt like an outsider, even in his own family. He'd never wanted to be a doctor, but that was expected of an Addison. When he'd returned to Pinecrest, all those years of trying to fit in and not succeeding came back and ate at him. Then Marcie and he had started going out. She'd been the one who wanted to keep it a secret. He'd wanted to parade her around, shouting to the townspeople Marcie Morgan was finally giving him the time of day.

Marcie's last journal had been with the photos of her in his closet. He admitted to reading some of it and realized that Marcie was playing with him. He was her amusement in an unhappy life. He'd begun following her and had seen her meeting Evan at the cabin.

Through all of this, Kira had seen another side to Marcie. A self-destructive one.

Pinecrest wasn't the same town through adult eyes. As a child, Kira had been naïve and easily swayed. She'd come a long way partially due to a bad marriage to Jonathan. She now knew what she wanted and intended to fight for it. Bill told her that the Morgans were back from Florida, which meant Gabriel was. She would go see him and make him aware of how much she wanted to be in his life.

"Kira, wait up a second." Bill strode to her. "Do you believe what Craig said about the murders? Especially about Mary Lou."

"Yes. Why would he lie?"

"To evade a fifth conviction of murder."

"What's one more when you'd be in prison for life or on death row?"

Bill's mouth twisted in a frown. "You're not surprised. Why not?"

"Because Mary Lou never totally fit with the other three. With Craig confessing to Marcie, Rebecca, and Shirley's deaths but not to Mary Lou's, we should leave her murder open. Something else is going on."

"That's what I was afraid of. We'll talk later."

She left the police station and nearly ran into Gabriel on the sidewalk. "What are you doing here?" was all she could think to say.

He smiled. "I came to see you. Your grandmother told me you were here. Did Craig confess and save the town a long trial?"

"Yes."

"Good. You and I need to talk."

"Here?" Kira looked around, pulling her coat together. "It's starting to snow in case you haven't noticed." A snowflake caught on her eyelashes. She blinked.

"I have my truck back. I'm so glad Jeremy's recovering."

"He shouldn't be working though."

"He didn't put my windshield and windows in. His employee did. My truck is still warm. Let's sit in it."

"You don't want to find a place in the police station."

"No. I don't want to see the inside of that building again." Gabriel put his hand at the small of her back and led her to the parking lot. Warmth still lingered inside his truck, but Gabriel switched on his engine and turned up the heater. "Is that better?"

"Yes. What do you want to talk about?" Hope blossomed in her heart.

"First this."

He bridged the short space between them and cupped her face. When he brushed his mouth across hers, the urge to throw her arms around him and demand more was strong. But she held back, needing to see what he wanted.

He didn't disappoint her. He nibbled her bottom lip then drew her toward him, pulling her into his embrace while he claimed a deep kiss that washed away any doubts Kira had about his feelings.

"I want to get to know you when we aren't fighting for our lives. I want to go out on dates like normal couples, share family time, and see where these feelings of love lead us. When I was in Craig's basement, all I wanted to do was escape and protect you. I didn't want to lose you."

"You won't because I want the same thing. I've seen you at your worst and best, and I love what I've seen. This is the first

Christmas in a long time that I'm really looking forward to, especially with you in it."

"That's the way I feel. Jessie wants to start decorating today. Want to join us?"

"I'd love to if you'll help me and Grams do the same. We only have a week, and she has big plans."

"I like how your grandmother thinks."

Kira finally wrapped her arms around Gabriel and kissed him as though she never wanted to leave his embrace. And she didn't.

Dear Reader,

Thank you for reading *Deadly Noel*, the fifth book in the **Strong Women, Extraordinary Situations**. This story about an assistant DA sending the wrong man to prison has been something I've wanted to write for years. I'm working on the sixth book in the series called *Deadly Dose* about who killed Mary Lou. She wasn't the serial killer's victim in *Deadly Noel*, so who killed her? Jessie Michaels is determined to find out. Look for *Deadly Dose* in the spring.

Take care,
Margaret

About the Author

Bestselling author, Margaret Daley, is multi-published with over 90 titles and 5 million books sold worldwide. She had written for Harlequin, Abingdon, Kensington, Dell, and Simon and Schuster. She has won multiple awards, including the prestigious Carol Award, Holt Medallion and Inspirational Readers' Choice Contest.

She has been married for over forty years and has one son and four granddaughters. When she isn't traveling, she's writing love stories, often with a suspense thread and corralling her three cats that think they rule her household.

To find out more about Margaret visit her website at *http://www.margaretdaley.com*.

Excerpt from
DEADLY DOSE
Book 6

The sound of the door clicking shut reverberated through Mary Lou's bedroom as Jessie Michaels stood in the middle of it and slowly rotated, taking in her best friend's possessions that Rebecca, Mary Lou's mother, had begged her to box up. Jessie hadn't wanted to, but Rebecca hadn't been able to go through Mary Lou's belongings for the past two months since her daughter was murdered.

"How am I going to do it?" Jessie whispered in the silence. A lump lodged in her throat, preventing her from talking any louder. The pain wasn't going away. She missed Mary Lou every day.

The sorrow and anger at Mary Lou's senseless death held Jessie paralyzed and unable to make the first step to fulfill Rebecca's plea.

Evidence of the Pinecrest police searching through her best friend's items sent a surge of anger and bitterness through Jessie. She didn't have any faith in them being able to solve Mary Lou's murder. It had been two months, and yet the police had discovered nothing other than she hadn't been one of the victims taken by the serial killer who had plagued the town last year. At least he was going to prison for viciously slaying four people. But someone had wanted Mary Lou's death to look like one of the killer's causalities.

Who?

For her own sanity, Rebecca wanted to pack up the house and move away from Pinecrest. Jessie didn't think her friend's mother would do anything with this room but shut the door to avoid all the painful memories. That left Jessie to help her. Rebecca had no one else.

Jessie sank onto the bed. Where should she start first? Her gaze lit upon the closet door ajar. A strong urge to begin there overwhelmed her, and she finally pushed herself to her feet and covered the distance to a cardboard box that Rebecca had brought in to use for Mary Lou's belongings.

Jessie took one and swung the closet door wide. The clothes hung neatly on the rod. She fingered a leather jacket that Mary Lou had saved six months to buy. Working as a cashier at the grocery store barely left money for any extras, especially since she helped her mother with her bills. Jessie removed the black coat from the hanger and brought it to her face. As if a bouquet of roses had been used in its construction, the soft leather still held a light scent of Mary Lou's favorite perfume.

Tears swelled in Jessie's eyes. She shut them. She didn't want to cry anymore. She'd never get the job done.

After quickly folding the jacket, she placed it in the cardboard box and went to the next piece of clothing. Twenty minutes later, the rod only held the hangers.

When Jessie sat on the floor to begin going through the shoes, her attention focused onto the baseboard on her left. Mary Lou's secret hiding place. She'd only shown Jessie the spot where she kept prize possessions to protect them in case they were ever robbed. Jessie pried the six-inch wooden board from its tight fit. Mary Lou had cut out a space in the wall containing a flat box for her special items.

Jessie wiggled it from the hole and lifted the lid. On top lay an envelope that had Jessie's name on it. Her hand trembled as she picked it up and turned it over. Sealed.

Why did she write *her* a letter? That wasn't like Mary Lou.

She almost stuffed it back in the box, put the lid on and set it aside for Rebecca. Almost. But Mary Lou made it a point to write to her. She had to know why.

Her hands still shaking, Jessie carefully tore one end off and slid the sheet of paper out. The sight of Mary Lou's beautiful handwriting jumped out at Jessie, and it took her a few seconds to focus on the words written by her best friend.

Jessie, if you're reading this, that means I'm dead...

Coming in the spring of 2016

DEADLY HUNT

Book 1 in
Strong Women, Extraordinary Situations
by Margaret Daley

All bodyguard Tess Miller wants is a vacation. But when a wounded stranger stumbles into her isolated cabin in the Arizona mountains, Tess becomes his lifeline. When Shane Burkhart opens his eyes, all he can focus on is his guardian angel leaning over him. And in the days to come he will need a guardian angel while being hunted by someone who wants him dead.

DEADLY INTENT

Book 2 in
Strong Women, Extraordinary Situations
by Margaret Daley

Texas Ranger Sarah Osborn thought she
would never see her high school
sweetheart, Ian O'Leary, again. But fifteen
years later, Ian, an ex-FBI agent, has
someone targeting him, and she's assigned
to the case. Can Sarah protect Ian and her
heart?

DEADLY HOLIDAY

Book 3 in
Strong Women, Extraordinary Situations
by Margaret Daley

Tory Caldwell witnesses a hit-and-run, but when the dead victim disappears from the scene, police doubt a crime has been committed. Tory is threatened when she keeps insisting she saw a man killed and the only one who believes her is her neighbor, Jordan Steele. Together, can they solve the mystery of the disappearing body and stay alive?

DEADLY COUNTDOWN

Book 4 in
Strong Women, Extraordinary Situations
by Margaret Daley

Allie Martin, a widow, has a secret protector who manipulates her life without anyone knowing until...

When Remy Broussard, an injured police officer, returns to Port David, Louisiana to visit before his medical leave is over, he discovers his childhood friend, Allie Martin, is being stalked. As Remy protects Allie and tries to find her stalker, they realize their feelings go beyond friendship.

When the stalker is found, they begin to explore the deeper feelings they have for each other, only to have a more sinister threat come between them. Will Allie be able to save Remy before he dies at the hand of a maniac?

Made in the USA
Lexington, KY
10 December 2015